THE FUTURE
MRS. DARCY

Given Good Principles

Vol. 2

Presented to

Kingwood Branch Library

WITHDRAWN

By

**FOLK – Friends of the Library
Kingwood**

Published by: Good Principles Publishing

The Future Mrs. Darcy

Copyright © 2012 Maria Grace

All rights reserved.

ISBN: 0615675050

ISBN-13: 978-0615675053

Author's Website: AuthorMariaGrace.com

Email address: Author.MariaGrace@gmail.com

GOOD PRINCIPLES
P U B L I S H I N G

DEDICATION

For my husband and sons who have always believed in me.

ACKNOWLEDGMENTS

So many people have helped me along the journey taking this from an idea to a reality. My greatest thanks to Lisa, Matt and Debra Anne, my original betas and cheering section Barb, Kathryn, Jan, Linnea, and Gayle you've kept me going and helped more than I can say. And my dear friend Cathy whose interest and support has kept me from chickening out more than once! Thank you!

CHAPTER 1

Early Spring, 1812

It is a truth universally acknowledged that wherever men in red coats gather, foolish young women follow.

The militia regiment had arrived in Meryton a week ago, and it was high time for them to be introduced to the community. The mayor, Sir William Lucas, well known among his neighbors for his love of good society and a good meal, liked nothing better than to make introductions. His parlor provided the ideal location for the officers to make a good impression.

Lydia bounced and chattered more than usual during the ride to Lucas Lodge, a difficult thing to accomplish with all six Bennet ladies squeezed into the coach at once. Elizabeth had offered to walk and allow them additional space.

"No, Lizzy, I do not want you seen arriving on foot. Besides, your petticoats would be six inches deep in mud by the time you arrived. I insist you ride with the rest of your sisters." Mrs. Bennet finished with a flourish that meant the discussion was indeed over.

When the coachman finally handed her out of the carriage, Elizabeth hid her sigh of relief in a discreet, ladylike cough. Mama shepherded Kitty and Lydia ahead of her and scolded them for being so long at their dressing tables that the Carvers had arrived before them. Jane and Mary followed at a less anxious pace. Elizabeth lagged behind and shook out her skirts, more to enjoy a brief moment of silence than to repair the state of her gown.

Mr. Bennet dismounted his horse and passed the reins to the driver. "Perhaps you ought to offer to ride Bessie next time. You would escape the carriage, and your petticoats would remain clean." He straightened his top hat and offered her his arm.

"I hardly believe Mama considers the smell of horse more fashionable than muddy skirts." She took his elbow and leaned her head on his shoulder.

He patted her hand. "If you say so, dear."

The modest parlor of Lucas Lodge, papered and painted in the style of years gone by, brimmed with guests. Sir William stood at the center of the room. His welcoming voice and laugh, both a fuzzy *basso profundo* rumble, filled the air. Young ladies surrounded him: Kitty, Lydia, his youngest daughter, Maria, and the fashionably dressed Carver sisters, Martha and Rachel.

"I dare say this will be a memorable season for Lydia." Mr. Bennet turned to Elizabeth with a raised eyebrow. "First, the Carvers take Netherfield." The corner of his lips rose ever so slightly. "I never thought to encounter another girl as silly as your youngest sister, and lo, not one, but two move into the neighborhood. Now the regiment camps among us. Any more excitement and she will be in danger of apoplexy."

A wry smile crept over Elizabeth's face. "Mama appears quite content. I daresay, Lydia shall be able to bear it as well." Her brow quirked, and her eyes flickered toward Mama in the far corner of the room, deep in conference with Lady Lucas and Aunt Phillips.

"You should go on, have your share of introductions while I partake of Sir William's library. He recently received a new collection that I am most anxious to examine." He winked and walked away.

She scanned the room.

Mary stood near the pianoforte and talked with Mr. Pierce, the hawk-nosed curate whose velvet voice left young ladies sighing. Her eyes glittered, adding volume to her quiet smile. Mary pulled her hair back a bit too tight and wore her collars a bit too high for most young men to pay attention to her. Only rarely did gentlemen take the time to speak with her. Mr. Pierce's popularity ensured others would soon interrupt, so Elizabeth sought other company.

Jane and Charlotte waved her over. She edged her way around the parlor.

"I thought I would not be able to make it across the room." Elizabeth sidled in close to Jane and Charlotte to clear the way for a scurrying maid. "Sir William has outdone himself tonight."

"You there, mind your step." Mr. Carver jumped aside. The punch glasses he carried in either hand nearly spilled.

Elizabeth cringed. Mr. Carver's nasal voice raised the hairs on the back of her neck. He moved like a portly heron, head bobbing forward and back, feet lifting a mite too high as he walked.

"Here." He pushed a cup at Jane's shoulder.

Jane blanched a bit and screwed her eyes shut. She blinked several times and turned to him with a paper-thin smile. "Thank you."

"I detest clumsy servants," he mumbled into his cup. "Gah, this is too sweet." He smacked his lips.

"I will inform my mother, sir." Charlotte nodded amiably, but a tiny "V" shaped crease deepened between her eyes.

"Be sure and do that. I wish to sit. Miss Bennet?" He took Jane by the elbow and guided her to a pair of chairs near the fireplace.

"At least his sisters are more agreeable." Elizabeth huffed. Her nostrils flared ever so slightly.

"Jane finds his company pleasant."

"She bears it well enough, I suppose, though I detect no symptoms of peculiar regard in her demeanor." Elizabeth pulled herself up and peered down her nose to ape any one of a number of women they both knew.

"Lizzy!" Charlotte snickered behind her hand. "He will hear you."

"Not likely. Look how he glowers at his sisters."

"They stand far too close to those officers." Charlotte's lips pulled tight. "At least Lydia and Maria keep a more proper distance."

Elizabeth rubbed the back of her neck. "I do not expect that to last very long."

Charlotte chewed her knuckle "No, it will not." She pointed her chin at the pianoforte.

Lydia skipped toward Mary, three lieutenants and an ensign in her wake. Kitty led a wave of young ladies behind them.

"I expect Mary will play a dance soon." Elizabeth wrinkled her nose.

"I thought you liked to dance."

"You know I am fond of dancing. It is having my toes trod upon I dread." Elizabeth glanced down and wiggled her foot towards the soldiers' boots. "Imagine the attack those hessians might wreak upon one's slippers."

Charlotte pressed the back of her hand to her mouth. She trembled with the effort to contain her amusement.

"Look at them, tripping over themselves to ask our sisters for a dance. Such grace does not bode well for a jig." The corner of Elizabeth's lips twitched.

Mary played a few chords while Rachel and Martha Carver directed the officers to roll up the carpet. Elizabeth and Charlotte dodged other guests who hurried off the hastily prepared dance floor. The couples took their places.

Only Lydia's partner showed any sense of rhythm. At least the others laughed heartily at their own missteps. A good sense of humor was a most desirable trait in a man, and essential for a clumsy one.

Carver did not share their amusement. He sat beside Jane, a deep scowl etched on his face. She squirmed and scuffed her slippers along the floor. Her cheeks tinged pink, not the pale blush of pleasure, but the ruddy glow of discomfiture. Jane needed rescue, so Elizabeth set off on her mission.

"—I do not understand why a knight like Sir William hosts these ruffians. I could easily do without the whole lot of them," Mr. Carver muttered into his fist.

Jane acknowledged Elizabeth with a quick nod. "Sir William is a great lover of company. To overlook—"

"Stuff and nonsense." Carver flicked his fingers. "I will not condone their presence at Netherfield's ball next month. The regiment is most assuredly not invited."

"Are you not concerned with giving offense?" The color crept from Jane's cheeks up her temples and down along her jaw.

"A man may do as he chooses in his own home. You cannot mean to say—"

"Excuse me." Elizabeth tucked herself between their chairs to accommodate a woman of ample proportions as she struggled to get past them. "Mr. Carver, might I steal my sister away for a few moments?"

He crossed his arms and tore his eyes from his sisters to peer narrowly at Elizabeth. "Certainly." He rose, bowed to Jane, and stalked into a knot of twittering young ladies.

"I do not envy them." Elizabeth took his seat. "He is quite severe on the Miss Carvers. If his face becomes any redder, I fear he may do himself an injury."

"His concern for them is not so terrible." Jane peeked over her shoulder.

"Do you suggest other young ladies might benefit from…stricter supervision?" Elizabeth followed Jane's gaze.

Lydia sat amongst three spellbound lieutenants who listened to her chatter. She granted them all pretty smiles and coquettish gazes. Kitty stood a few steps away with Maria. Both exerted themselves to gain the attention of an ensign whose eyes were firmly on Lydia.

"Are you not at all concerned?" Jane asked.

"Papa is not alarmed."

"Mr. Carver—"

"You cannot please everyone, Jane. Mr. Carver is the sort of man who will always be dissatisfied with something. Since everything displeases him, why be concerned with any of it?"

"But—"

"No, he is a curmudgeon. Even Papa says so. Do not take his complaints to heart." Elizabeth pulled Jane to her feet. "Come, Sir William wants to make introductions. It will not do to be rude to our neighbor even for Mr. Carver's sake. If the officers are a bit boorish, still, what harm is there in the acquaintance?"

CHAPTER 2

Late Spring, 1812

"Audacity! What else can you call it?" Elizabeth snapped a supple branch from an unlucky bush along the path up Oakham Mount. She whipped it through the air. The sharp whistle in its wake pleased her. "If I were a man, I would have called him out." The switch snapped through the leaves of the nearest shrub. Several flew into her face. "At least I may take comfort in his departure."

The humiliating conversation with Mr. Carver boxed her ears. They stung and rang with his voice. "How dare he say such things." She cracked the switch across her knee and threw it aside. "Kitty and Lydia are high spirited, but they are not hoydens."

Her bonnet slipped down and clung to her neck by its ribbons. Several curls fluttered in the breeze and tickled her cheeks. Grumbling under her breath, she shoved them behind her ears.

"One moment we are his invited guests, dancing with him at his private ball. Then the very next day, he turns me out like garbage." She threw her arms up to the sky.

A crow cawed to admonish her unladylike display.

"That is easy enough for you to say." She searched for the sassy bird. "You were not refused when you came to call."

Wind whipped stray hair into her eyes and jerked her bonnet hard against her throat.

Her voice dropped into a mocking baritone. "'I mean no offense. Nevertheless, I must get to the point, Miss Bennet. I cannot allow my sisters to continue in your acquaintance.'" She pulled her bonnet into place and tied the ribbons far too tightly. "He meant no offense to Jane or me? Obviously, our ladylike manners are insufficient in the face of the vulgarities of the rest of our family."

Her jaw ached and a headache threatened. "How dare he judge us when he cannot manage his own family. Rachel and Martha were far more boisterous than Kitty and Lydia. Yet he blames us for his sisters' mischief."

At the top of Oakham Mount, she dropped down on her favorite fallen log. Her father's estate painted the landscape below her with newly planted fields and pastures dotted with sheep. On the narrow road bordering Longbourn, a row of carriages trundled toward London. She bent and massaged her throbbing temples. At least Mama would cease her talk of a wedding. *I wish no ill on Mr. Bascomb, but I will rejoice if Netherfield remains vacant for quite some time.*

·•·❧❧·•·❧❧·•·❧❧·•·❧❧·•·❧❧·•·

Elizabeth dragged her feet up the front steps. Mama appeared in the window and energetically beckoned her inside. Yet another discussion of the Carvers would surely follow. She opened the door as slowly as possible.

"What do you make of this strange business at Netherfield, Lizzy?" Mama moaned and fanned her handkerchief. Her mobcap sagged down low and pushed a fringe of hair into her eyes.

"He is a wealthy man who exercised the privilege of affluence. He follows his whims of pleasure with little concern for the effects upon the neighborhood." She avoided Mama's scrutiny as best she could while she untied her bonnet, removed her wrap, and laid them on the hall table.

"Oh, the hopes we had for him. What a smart match for our dear Jane. He paid her such attentions." Mama dabbed her eyes. "Jane would have been a good influence on his sisters—they were so wild. Nothing like you girls."

Elizabeth cringed. If Mama had heard what Mr. Carver thought of her dearest girls, how different this conversation would be. A dull ache pounded in her head. She pulled a footstool closer and sat across from Mama.

"Will you never sit in a chair like a proper young lady? You do so enjoy trying my nerves." She pursed her lips and tapped her heel.

"I am sorry, Mama." Elizabeth looked down. A brief interview was hardly worthy of a chair.

Mama snorted a familiar disapproving huff. "Who can fathom their departure? I will always say he used my dear girl very ill indeed. She is left with a broken heart."

"Is Jane so affected?" Elizabeth leaned in closer, her brow furrowed. Surely Jane would not have kept something so significant from her.

"Your sister is longsuffering, but a mother understands. She grieves for what we will suffer when your father dies and his odious cousin throws us out into the hedgerows. If only we had produced a son."

"But Jane and Mr. Carver had no understanding between them."

She patted Elizabeth's knee and shook her head. "Jane would not be so beautiful unless her destiny was to marry well and save us all."

"Mama—"

"Do not take that tone with me, young lady. You may not like to hear it, but Jane failed us by not securing Mr. Carver. There is little hope *you* will be the saving of us."

Elizabeth's heart pinched. She steeled herself for yet another reminder that beauty alone—not intelligence, character, resourcefulness or any trait Papa might endorse—would save the family.

Mama launched her familiar monologue, one that Elizabeth could quote word for word. Despite the many times she had heard it, this repetition hurt no less than the previous. Her eyes stung. She blinked furiously. If she did not concentrate on something other than Mama's disappointment in her, tears would fall and make things even worse. Did Jane actually want Mr. Carver's attentions? That was a worthy consideration.

"Lizzy." Mama grabbed Elizabeth's forearm. "Did you hear me? Do not speak of it to Jane. She suffers enough." Mama sniffled, pressed her handkerchief to her nose, and turned to the window.

Summarily dismissed, Elizabeth rose and scooted the footstool into its proper place.

Kitty's high-pitched shriek shattered the air. "Lydia. Give me my bonnet."

Lydia burst into the room, hat in hand. The ribbons flew behind as she dashed through the room. "Mama! Mama!"

"Make her give it back." Kitty struggled to snatch it away. She stamped her foot and crossed her arms, shoulders pulled high around her ears.

"She has never even worn the ugly thing." Lydia pouted at her mother and leveled a narrow glare at Kitty.

"That is not fair." Kitty stamped again. Her fists shook at her sides. "Lizzy, tell Mama. You went to the milliner's with me to make the purchase. " The word ended in a shriek and another grab for the headgear. "It is mine."

Elizabeth winced. Kitty's needle-sharp voice jabbed her temples. "I am sorry." She clutched her head. "I cannot today. You must settle this dispute without me." She pushed away protests with an open hand. "Pray excuse me."

Lydia and Kitty resumed their argument as Elizabeth trudged upstairs to the small dressing room she and Jane shared.

Jane met her at the doorway. She took Elizabeth's arm and led her to a worn, blue brocade chair. "Headache?"

"A ghastly one." Elizabeth sat and pulled her knees under her chin.

Tortured strains of pianoforte music filtered in from the drawing room.

"I do not need one of Mary's concertos now." Elizabeth grumbled. She hid her face in her hands.

"You are too harsh on her. She plays to drown out Kitty and Lydia's quarrels."

"Does she have to choose something she cannot even play well?"

Jane's eyes narrowed, and her lips pressed into a tight line.

"Forgive me, that was ungracious. This headache has stolen my good humor."

"You should take time to talk with Mary." Jane wandered to the window seat and retrieved her needlework.

"She is forever sermonizing. Do you truly wish to listen to her quote Fordyce and whomever else she has recently read?"

"You do the very same thing with the latest philosophers and poets you read."

Elizabeth harrumphed and bounced back against the chair.

"Yes, you do. Be fair now. Ouch." Jane winced and stuffed her finger in her mouth. "I cannot stop jabbing myself when I do this new stitch." She pulled her finger out and squeezed it.

"I think Kitty is the only one among us who manages without bloodshed. I never realized her embroidery skills until just last week."

"You would recognize Mary's proficiencies, too, if you took the time to talk with her. Her understanding is every bit as good as yours. We do not get to benefit from it because she is shy and cannot tolerate Papa's teasing with aplomb like you."

A cold ache filled Elizabeth's belly. Jane never scolded. She joined Jane at the window. "Are you well?"

Jane shrugged and turned her face away.

"The Carvers?"

Jane's shoulder's twitched.

"You enjoyed your acquaintance with him?"

"I do not know." Jane traced her fingertip along the window casing, gathering bits of dust the maid had missed. She brushed them away with her thumb.

"Can you not hear your own heart, or are you afraid to listen to it?" Elizabeth laid her hand on Jane's shoulder. "Mama declared you must like him because of his wealth. What did your heart say?"

The window fogged with Jane's shallow breath. The haze retreated to be replaced by another as she breathed again.

"Tell me honestly, did you like Mr. Carver? I mean like him in the way you wish to like a…a husband?"

Jane bowed her head just enough so that her breath no longer kissed the windowpane. "To be entirely honest—and I would say this only to you—no, I did not."

Elizabeth rubbed her back gently.

"For a quarter of an hour in the drawing room, he was gentlemanly and agreeable enough. In his company for longer periods, though, I found his manner coarse, gruff, and quite unpleasant."

"You look like you did the day you walked with me and got sand in your shoes. You would not stop to shake them out. It tortured you all the way home." Elizabeth snickered. "I should not laugh for I know you were miserable, but your face."

"That is exactly how he made me feel. He grated on my nerves, but in small ways: how he called after his sisters, his tone with his servants. Oh, and the way he held his knife and fork at the table—it was all I could do not to remove them from his hands and show him the right way." Jane's fingers twitched. "Nothing I might justly complain about, nothing that Mama would understand anyway." She sighed and dropped her chin to her chest. "If anything, I am relieved they have left. I know it is selfish of me, and I should be sorry, but I am not."

Elizabeth squeezed her shoulder. "Mama feared you heartbroken, though I did not think you so touched by Mr. Carver."

"Not by him." Jane smiled.

Elizabeth recognized the expression. Jane was trying to make her feel better. It was not working.

"I regret I have disappointed Mama and failed to do my duty by all of you."

The knot in Elizabeth's stomach tightened. "You take too much upon yourself. Despite Mama's insistence, it is not in your power to provide for all of us. We must trust in Providence for that." She played with the stray curls at the back of Jane's neck.

"Ever the font of wisdom, Lizzy." Jane's lips wrinkled into a funny little half frown. "I am conscience stricken to admit I am relieved it is over. He did not keep his sentiments to himself and had a mean opinion of our family." She held her hand up. "No, do not object so quickly. He was quite clear he found nothing to reproach in you, but of our sisters and parents—that was another matter."

"I think him a hypocrite, given the behavior of his own sisters and the poor control he showed over his family." Elizabeth walked to the fireplace and leaned on the mantle. She ran her fingers along the edge of a small Blue Onion vase.

"I have often wondered if he was correct about Kitty and Lydia." Jane shifted and plucked at her skirts, eventually smoothing them over her knees. "He even called Mary boring with all her morality and self-control."

Elizabeth's hand jerked. She nearly knocked the vase off the mantle and jumped to catch it. "A man who complains that one is too lively and another is too good will never be pleased. I suppose we should thank our sisters. You are freed from the burden of rejecting a suitor you did not like." She cocked her head and wagged her brows.

"Do you think he might be right about Lydia, and even Kitty?" Jane frowned and picked up her needlework. "They are so boisterous—"

"Only you would attempt to take his opinions to heart. I am still utterly convinced he was wrong." Elizabeth chewed the inside of her cheek to drive away the tiny seed of doubt, or was that her headache redoubling its attack?

Jane drew a deep breath, squared her shoulders and lifted her chin. "Does your head still hurt? You should lie down for a while."

"Since the concerto is over and the parlor is quiet, I think I will." Elizabeth stopped to squeeze Jane's hand and shuffled to her room.

Jane's discreet concern alarmed her more than Mama's raucous distress, but she would deal with that after the pain subsided. If it ever did.

Several hours later, stomach pangs replaced the throbbing in her head and drove Elizabeth from her room. Silence filled the halls, a noteworthy event at Longbourn. The fragrance of fresh bread lured her to the parlor.

"Good afternoon to you, Lizzy dear." Papa winked.

"Good afternoon." Elizabeth kissed his cheek.

"You were sorely missed at breakfast."

She laughed and served herself. "I fear what you mean to say is you missed your ally in 'sensible' conversation." Plate in hand, she sat beside him, on a chair, and Mama was not even there to approve. "How do we have the drawing room to ourselves?"

"I am afraid the departure of the Carvers left your mother with a great many tremblings and flutterings. So many, in fact, they require the solace offered by an afternoon's visit with her sister Phillips. How she should soothe anyone, I shall never comprehend." He snorted and slicked butter over a slice of bread. "Kitty and Lydia accompanied her with high hopes of sighting an officer or two."

Her mouth dried up. A bite of cheese crumbled into tasteless dust on her tongue. "I expect they will miss the company of the Miss Carvers."

"You may be right." He chuckled, brushing crumbs from his fingertips. "I did not believe two girls as silly as your younger sisters existed in all of England. Yet, somehow they found their way into Hertfordshire."

"Are you not troubled to hear Lydia and Kitty counted with girls of such character?" Elizabeth caught her bottom lip between her teeth.

"You worry far too much, dear." He flicked the suggestion away like a fly. "For what do we live, but to make sport for our neighbors and laugh at them in our turn? They are young and silly. Fear not, neither you, nor Jane, nor even Mary, shall ever be classed with them. No harm will come of their frivolities. I am certain." He leaned a little closer and squinted. "The Carvers' departure has not vexed you, too?"

She opened her mouth and closed it again, shaking her head. His reassurance should have made her feel better. Still, relief remained just beyond her fingertips. "No, Papa. I believe my headache left me unsettled, that is all."

"You ought to take a walk after lunch. The weather is fine, and the sunshine will help you find yourself again." He glanced at the doorway.

She followed his gaze.

Mary stood in the doorway, indecisive and shy.

"You did not go into town too? I thought you wished to visit the circulating library." Elizabeth waved her in.

Mary mouthed the word "no" and shuffled to the sideboard for a plate. She chose a chair opposite Elizabeth and away from Papa. "They went into town in search of gossip and officers," she murmured, eyes on her plate.

"You do not approve." Papa did not look up from the slabs of meat and cheese he sliced to fit across a piece of bread.

Mary's shoulders slumped.

Elizabeth wondered if she always did that when Papa spoke to her. As she thought on it, it was quite possible Mary did.

"Loss of virtue in a female is irretrievable—one false step involves her in endless ruin—for her reputation is no less brittle than it is beautiful. I believe one cannot be too much guarded in her behavior towards the undeserving of the other sex." Mary shrank further into her chair.

"So, you are afraid your sisters' virtue—and yours— will be ruined by their silly flirtations? Silliness is a far cry from ruination. Do not make more of this than you ought. Walk into town today and see for yourselves. You have no reason for concern." He brushed his hands together over his plate and laid his napkin on top of the empty china. "I will leave you to your journey." He rose, placed the dish on the sideboard and left.

Mary followed Papa with her eyes but said nothing. With a sad sigh, she returned to her meal.

The silence in the room expanded, pressing on Elizabeth until she fought to breathe. She must speak, but what could she say that would not further upset Mary? Two shallow breaths passed. "You do not agree with Papa?"

Mary's head lifted sharply. She stared, mouth agape, and blinked three times.

Elizabeth pressed her palm to her cheek. Why did Mary look at her that way? Had she never asked Mary her opinion before? Maybe she had not. *Oh, dear.* "You seem very concerned."

Mary looked down, her voice barely above a whisper. "I have recently noticed some of our neighbors never seem to be home anymore when Lydia calls. I called upon several of those same families, and they are not home to me either. I do not know what to make of it."

Cold prickles scoured Elizabeth's face. "How singular. Whom did you try to call upon? I will visit them myself—"

"I do not wish to gossip or poison you against other families needlessly." Mary pulled off a small piece of bread and put it in her mouth.

Elizabeth tried to catch her eyes, but Mary looked away. "You are right."

Mary offered no comment.

The small sounds of eating and the mantle clock's ticking grew unbearably loud, threatening to deafen her. "What say you we make a trip into town as Papa suggested? I should like to go to the library with you."

Mary stared wide-eyed until Elizabeth nodded. "I will get my bonnet." She flashed a rare smile.

As they walked, Elizabeth prodded Mary to talk. Though hesitant at first, she slowly opened up. For her part, Elizabeth schooled herself to listen with the same patience she accorded Papa. The effort, she noted with some chagrin, proved a worthy one, as she came to agree with Jane. Mary spoke much good sense.

About a mile from town, they encountered Charlotte and Maria Lucas struggling with a heavy basket.

"Here, Maria, let me help you." Elizabeth rushed to Maria.

"Thank you ever so much, Lizzy." Maria released the handle to Elizabeth and shook her hands vigorously.

Mary helped Charlotte with the other side and peered into the basket. "Where are you taking such a large load?"

"To one of the Netherfield cottagers," Charlotte said.

"Who is sick?" Mary asked.

"How do you know someone is unwell?" Elizabeth looked at Mary. "And why Netherfield tenants?" She turned to Charlotte.

"Packets of cherry bark and willow bark and a small jar of honey." Mary pointed them out. "Someone suffers with a cough and sore throat, and I am not sure what else."

Elizabeth's brows rose.

"The herbs help those symptoms." Mary tucked her face into her shoulder, cheeks bright.

"Mary visits Mama at least twice a week. Mama has been teaching her about herbs for close to a year now." Maria bobbed on her toes and wore a tattletale smile.

Mary's ears reddened as she glared at Maria.

Elizabeth stared slack-jawed. She shut her mouth with a sharp click of her teeth. Jane was right. She definitely needed to talk with Mary more.

"Not everyone can afford an apothecary's preparations." Mary shrugged.

"Like the Blacks, who live in the smallest cottage on Netherfield Park. Their farm did not produce well this year, and every one of them took ill during the winter," Charlotte said.

Elizabeth still stared at Mary.

"They should be Mr. Bascomb's responsibility." Maria frowned, arms crossed over her chest. She edged away from the others.

"Maria does not enjoy these charitable visits. You must excuse her." Charlotte glowered like Hill at a recalcitrant scullery maid. "When my father kept shop, our mother always cared for his employees. Now, she misses the opportunity for works of charity and attends to the less fortunate of our neighbors."

"Mr. Bascomb is a most neglectful landlord if you ask me." Maria flipped her bonnet's ribbons.

Charlotte rolled her eyes. "Mrs. Black is seriously ill right now, and her eldest daughter is not more than seven years old. Her mother-in-law stays with them to help though it means another body at the dinner table."

"I do not understand why Mama must seek charity cases for us to spend our time on." She pouted and flounced exactly as Lydia did when she did not get her way. "Do not look at me like that, Charlotte."

"Just because you think something does not give you leave to speak your mind," Charlotte hissed. "Show some decorum, Maria."

"No one thinks well of Mr. Bascomb." Maria stomped. A small cloud of dust enveloped her foot. "Mrs. Lawton said she thought there was no Mrs. Bascomb because—"

"Maria!"

Elizabeth winced at Charlotte's sharp tone, but Maria appeared unaffected.

Mary slowly fixed her scrutiny on Maria who dug her toes into the dirt. "Did you not hear Mr. Pierce's sermon last Sunday?"

"He was ever so severe." Maria bowed her head.

"Gossip is not a suitable pursuit for a lady. How dare you judge another who is not even here to defend himself. What is more, do you want others talking about you—"

"Oh, Mary, not another sermon." Maria harrumphed and crowded her shoulders to her ears. "Leave that for the curate on Sunday. There is little enough harm in such idle talk. I am certain they must speak about us just as much as we do them. I do not see what is so bad."

Charlotte cringed and bounced her gaze from Maria to Elizabeth. "Perhaps you should not come with me to the Blacks' today."

"I had planned to meet Kitty and Lydia in town this afternoon before Mama devised this errand for us." Maria blinked big pleading eyes.

"Go, I will meet you at home."

Before Charlotte could say any more, Maria took off.

"We were only going to the library." Mary glanced at Elizabeth who nodded. "May we accompany you instead?"

"Thank you, I would like that." Charlotte blinked slowly. "I apologize for Maria's thoughtlessness."

"It is nothing. Lydia would have been equally put out. Do not be concerned." Elizabeth offered a smile, but Charlotte rejected it. "What is wrong?"

Charlotte jerked her head toward a fallen log. They left the basket near the path and sat on the log. She propped her elbows on her knees and pressed her forehead on her knuckles. "There are those who say Mr. Carver declared the society in Meryton something savage and felt his sisters materially damaged by their acquaintances here."

Elizabeth held her breath. Where had Charlotte heard that?

"What a harsh judgment upon our neighborhood," Mary said.

"The judgment may be far more personal than that."

"Maria?" Elizabeth sat a little straighter and leaned forward to catch Charlotte's eye.

"Yes, Maria." Her gaze flickered from Elizabeth to Mary and back again. "You have not noticed a change in her behavior since the regiment arrived?"

"No, I have not." Elizabeth brushed her knuckles along her chin.

Charlotte puffed a breath through her cheeks. "I find that difficult to believe from you, who are such a great observer of people's absurdities." A small piece of bark broke off in her fingers, and she threw it aside. "It started the night my father introduced the officers. Every day since, Maria has become more boisterous and even flirtatious. She talks of little but the officers. I can no longer check her energies." She pinched the bridge of her nose. "I loath the thought, but I must discuss this with my mother. How am I to tell her I believe my sister drove our neighbors away with her indecent behavior?" She covered her face with her hands.

"Papa believes their youthful exuberance is harmless and will come to nothing." Elizabeth chewed her bottom lip.

"Perhaps for you and your sisters. Your father is a gentleman. Despite his knighthood, my father's ties to trade are very recent. My prospects are meager enough." Charlotte rubbed her sleeve across her face. "Just yesterday, I overheard Mrs. Long criticizing Maria to Mrs. Bond."

"What will you tell Lady Lucas?" Elizabeth struggled to ignore the heat prickling at the back of her neck—or was that her conscience?

"I do not know. It is not the conversation a daughter is supposed to have with her mother. She should admonish me, not I her." She peeked over her fingertips.

"Perhaps your sister is not the one whom Mr. Carver found so objectionable. There are many young ladies in town." Elizabeth cocked her head at Mary, who dropped her eyes.

"Is it not enough her behavior could earn her such censure whether or not she was indeed the cause? With all of her carrying on, Maria has nearly lost her delicacy. If that happens, her reputation, and mine by extension, will be irretrievable. We will have no hope of making any kind of match, and be forever dependent upon the kindness of our brothers—maiden aunts to care for their children. Though I am nearly on the shelf, I still hoped..." Charlotte hid herself in her lap and wept.

Elizabeth chewed the inside of her cheek. Papa often praised her discernment, but if Maria's behavior, which had never attracted her notice, was so far gone that unflappable Charlotte was distraught, could she trust her own judgment? How would she know? Mr. Carver could not have been correct, could he? A knot of dread tied itself in her belly.

CHAPTER 3

Elizabeth woke, panting and panicked from the disaster—wait, was that thunder? She untangled herself from her sheets and sat up in a room lit by random flashes of lightning. What a terrible dream—no a nightmare. She clutched the sheets in shaky fists and reveled in the knowledge Lydia had not run away with Farmer Clay's son and killed Papa with the shock; no cousin on the way to cast them all into the snow; no Mr. Carver on their doorstep, laughing at their plight.

Her heart settled into a reasonable pace, beating in time to the raindrops' *tink-tink-tink* on the windowpane. One deep breath, then another, and calm filtered into her limbs. She sank into her pillow to blink away the burn in her eyes.

Several blinks later, dawn forced its way through her window and slid past her closed eyelids. No point in trying to sleep further. She needed a walk.

Elizabeth found the mud puddles easier to dodge than the lingering concerns from her talk with Charlotte. By the time she returned to the house, a sick knot had lodged just below her ribs and invited itself to stay for breakfast.

Surely a chat with Papa would dismiss it. She found him at the breakfast table, plate untouched, his face buried in the most recent newspaper.

Papa peered over the edge of his paper. "Good morning, Lizzy. Did you enjoy your walk?"

"I did, though not as much as in drier weather." She smiled ruefully and lifted her dirty skirt hem away from muddy boots.

"You ought to avoid Hill until you change your dress, my dear. She is in high dudgeon this morning." He folded the newspaper with a snap and tucked it alongside his plate.

"Whatever for? Hill is usually the embodiment of everything patient." Lizzy served herself from the sideboard and joined him.

"I fear even she has reached her limit. After your sisters came home from town yesterday, they were embroiled in some sort of quarrel in the stillroom and upended or unsettled something or other. I do not recall whether soap, or fragrance, or perhaps jelly Hill was setting up." His hand fluttered in the air. "Whatever—it was ruined."

2

"Oh, no. All her hard work—" Elizabeth screwed her eyes shut. "I will be sure to stay out of her way today."

"I would advise it, lest you be recruited to help repair the damages."

"That might not be so bad a fate, unless it was a batch of soap. I never get the lye mixture quite right. My soaps are always too thick."

"In that case, be sure to make breakfast a quick affair." He winked and sipped his coffee. "I am glad you have regained your normal equanimity. I could hardly fathom Carver's departure affected you so."

"No, it did not, but—"

He leaned to his right to look past Elizabeth and through the front windows. "That is Phillips' gig."

"You are expecting him?" She pressed a hand to her belly. What a time for visitors to arrive. Now Papa would not have time to talk until evening, a long time to entertain the growing knot in her side.

"I am, just not this early." He scowled. "Your aunt has come with him. I did not expect *her.*" He rose and grumbled unintelligible syllables from deep in his throat. "You will excuse me." His normally soft footfalls turned to stomps when he left the room.

Why did he have to be called away now when she needed his reassurance? Perhaps more troubling, why did Aunt Phillips visit so early? She stared at her plate, and her stomach pinched.

Footsteps sounded on the stairs—her sisters. Perhaps a little time with them would soothe her disquiet.

And perhaps Napoleon would come to the door to invite her to tea.

· •ঔৈ৽· • ·ঔৈ৽· • ·ঔৈ৽· • ·ঔৈ৽· • ·ঔৈ৽· • ·

Bennet opened the door into the narrow foyer before Phillips bruised his knuckles on the weathered oak. "I am glad you are come, David." He shook his brother-in-law's hand.

He took his time to acknowledge Mrs. Phillips, far longer than considered polite. Graciousness was difficult when she reminded him of old Mrs. Gardiner, prattling and tattling like a gaggle of geese.

She shuffled her feet and peeked at him expectantly. They had done this dance before.

Bennet pulled himself to his full height and scrutinized her. "I did not expect you, Edith."

"I simply had to visit Fanny. She was so distraught yesterday. I have something to tell her that will make her feel better. Besides, she left her vinaigrette[1] at my house. The chain from her chatelaine [2] broke." She held it up.

---

[1] Vinaigrette: A small container with a perforated top, used to contain an aromatic substance such as vinegar or smelling salts.
[2] Chatelaine: A decorative belt hook or clasp worn at the waist with a series of chains suspended from it. Each chain held a useful household gadget such as scissors, thimble, watch, key, vinaigrette, household seal, etc.

How was it, she managed to use fifty words when five would suffice? Bennet drew out his glasses and examined the small filigree box with far more care than required.

She squirmed and ran her finger inside her collar.

He smiled thinly and tucked the spectacles into his pocket. "Fanny has not yet come downstairs."

"I will be happy to go upstairs." She hopped toward the stairs.

Bennet caught her by the elbow. "Edith…"

"I understand, Thomas." She bobbed her head, avoiding his eyes.

With a glance, he conferred with Phillips, who nodded, more reluctantly than Bennet preferred. He released her, and she dashed up the stairs.

The two men stood for a moment.

Knuckles rapped on a door that squeaked opened.

"Sister." Fanny and Edith cried.

The door shut firmly.

"Sisters will always find something to talk about. My two eldest sisters still talk one another under the table after nigh on sixty years now." Phillips raised an open hand. "I warned her before we left."

Bennet muttered and rubbed his fist along his chin. "Come, I have his last letter in my book room." He led the few steps into his study, Longbourn's only bastion of masculinity: piles and heaps and shelves of books, leather chairs, chess, port and brandy. He dropped into his favorite seat, the one whose lumps and bumps matched his own. "Coffee?"

"Not today. The bitterness does not agree with me so early in the morning." Phillips eased himself into a comfortably worn wingback, the stuffing barely visible in the thin spots where his elbows hit the chair arms.

Bennet reached across his desk and shoved aside a pile of books with his elbow. "Ah, here." He extracted a piece of paper and extended it to Phillips. The broken seal clung heroically to the edge, then fell off the paper, bounced on the faded carpet and rolled under the desk.

Phillips bent over the arm of the chair, reaching and grunting.

"Do not bother. It is satisfying to know part of him will be under my feet." Bennet waved him back. "The addle pate reminds me of Rawls."

"No wonder you were so thin-skinned with Edith." Phillips rolled his eyes.

Bennet hauled himself out of his chair and dodged the footstool and two stacks of books on his way to the window. There, he retrieved the brandy decanter and two glasses. He lifted them and Phillips nodded. "Fanny never truly recovered from Rawls's death."

Phillips shook his head and accepted the proffered crystal. "What a sad business."

"Have you any news of our eldest sister?" Bennet held the glass up to catch a sunbeam and eased into his chair. Chestnut flashes fractured in the snifter and ricocheted off the walls. He sipped the brandy. This particular bottle had just the right amount of burn along the back of his throat. "A mite early for this, I know."

6

"Not considering this." Phillips glanced at the letter. "Gardiner alone kept touch with her after Rawls's death. He has not mentioned her in well over a year now." He took a deep draw from his brandy and set it aside. "Enough of that, tell me of this letter." He unfolded the paper and moved it closer to his face, then farther away again. He gave up and fumbled for his spectacles. "His hand is utterly frightful. How did he graduate Cambridge?"

"I would be content if that were the only frightful thing about him." Bennet scowled.

"Father's death came as a surprise…" Phillips waved his hand, conducting his way through the scrawl, "…hardly feels up to dealing with all the legal ramifications thereof." He looked up. "While I am sorry for his loss—"

"Do not be." Bennet plucked his bifocals from his pocket and polished them with his handkerchief. "His father was an ignorant, miserly man. The world is better off without him."

"Such strong language." Phillips squinted at the letter again.

"That puts it mildly." Bennet balanced his glasses on his nose. Blasted things never did set quite right. "He fought me tooth and nail every time I sought to improve Longbourn. 'It is a waste' he would say and threaten to bring me to court." He raked his hair.

"So you allowed the estate to—"

"—to remain as I inherited it." He covered his eyes with his hand, smudging his spectacles afresh.

The memories remained strong: old debates, raised voices, ugly invectives, Fanny in a dither. Such were the gracious gifts of his oh-so-thoughtful cousin, Collins. Bennet growled through clenched teeth, face knotted into a wretched mask. He snatched a deep breath and held it. Twice more, and the knots in his jaw released.

One further and he found his voice. "I have never had the capital for improvements. He refused to allow me to mortgage it to obtain capital. The irony is he never understood those improvements would ultimately benefit his son." He beckoned toward the letter.

Phillips picked up a napkin from the table beside him and passed it with the letter.

Bennet mopped his face. "It is my daughters who must pay the price for his stinginess. Those improvements would have provided them decent dowries."

"You hope to convince young Collins to permit the mortgage?"

"What do you think this beastly ongoing exchange of letters has been about? I would not otherwise suffer a correspondence with him." Bennet rattled the paper and snapped it with his other hand. He would have liked to do that to Collins himself.

"Obviously the negotiations have not gone well." Phillips sipped his brandy.

"I expected a Cambridge education would leave him able to apprehend basic reasoning. Instead, he takes after his father, all stubbornness and no sense."

"I am surprised. You told me he obtained a generous living in Kent under a 'noble patroness.' Not many of that class tolerate a fool at their table."

"Collins is a sycophant, and I imagine that character of man appeals to some. No accounting for taste amongst higher levels of society." Bennet scratched his temple. "The problem is …" he held the letter up to the light and followed the lines with his fingertip, "here, he says he cannot possibly contemplate such a concession lightly. His so-called 'noble patroness' insists he visits the estate himself to determine whether or not such expenses are truly warranted." He folded the correspondence and wished for the chance to pinch the same creases in Collins's face. "I swear that man's brains are in his bollocks."

Phillips started and gasped, a twinkle in his eye. "Such language, Thomas."

"Do not go there." Bennet grumbled. "Allow me the privilege, if only for a moment, of speaking like a man."

"You are right. I should not tease you so. For all you have done for my sister, you deserve quarter from me."

"Fanny does not tolerate his kind of company in the house. I must go to Kent and try to dissuade him from visiting Longbourn. Lord knows I hate to travel, but I see no other way." He dropped the letter onto the desk. Burning it held greater appeal.

"Would it help if I accompanied you? At least that way, should he have a change of heart, I can draw up the papers immediately." Phillips reached for his glass. A shriek from upstairs stayed his hand midway.

"That was Fanny…" Bennet slammed his teeth hard enough he feared they might break and raced upstairs. What could that babbling prittle-prattle have said this time?

·•ॐ∽⃛·•·ॐ∽⃛·•·ॐ∽⃛·•·ॐ∽⃛·•·ॐ∽⃛•·

"How droll." Lydia laughed from the doorway, hands on her hips.

Kitty peeked over Lydia's head. "You look just like Papa hiding behind the paper."

"Good morning." Lizzy forced herself to smile. Why did reading draw such derision? Prickly remarks, caught like thistles in her throat. She washed them down with half a glass of water and a sigh.

They served themselves and sat, chattering in half sentences and veiled references to their trip to town.

"I am glad that horrid rain stopped." Lydia paused to take a large bite of her muffin and continued, mouth still full. "I was afraid we would be forced to stay home all day and die of boredom." Crumbs sprayed the tablecloth.

"Lyddie!" Lizzy handed her a napkin.

Lydia snatched it with a snort.

Kitty spread jam on her bread, careful to cover it entirely from edge to edge. "I cannot bear to spend all day at home." She looked at Lydia, and they giggled.

"I would not plan on going out. Papa believes Hill needs your assistance today—something about an accident in the still room." Elizabeth's brow rose, and she cocked her head.

"Hill is a chuffy old cross patch in need of something to scold about." Lydia bounced her fist on the table and pouted.

"We did not mean to knock over the soap molds." Kitty kept her eyes lowered and bit her lower lip. "She was able to scrape up what was spilled."

"But now the soap must be melted and strained and remolded." Elizabeth ticked the points off on her fingers.

"Servants are paid for such disagreeable tasks." Lydia wrinkled her nose and peeked at the empty doorway. "Mama would never expect us to do so."

"You should at least help since you caused so much damage."

"We planned to go to town." Kitty picked at a pulled thread on the tablecloth.

"You should…"

"No—"

A shriek from upstairs cut off their conversation.

Elizabeth's breath hitched. Her skin tingled as she struggled to make out other muffled sounds from the front of the house.

"Ooo, I saw Aunt Phillips going upstairs." Lydia rubbed her hands together. "She must have juicy gossip for Mama. I wonder if she—"

"Thank you, Lydia." Lizzy folded her napkin and laid it on the table. So much for any hope of holding her attention now. She turned her shoulder to Lydia and focused on Kitty. "I do not understand the urgency of your trip. You were in town yesterday. Why do you need to go again today?"

"We purchased the latest edition of The Lady's Magazine yesterday. The printed patterns...oh the sleeves." Kitty clapped lightly, and her eyes lit. "They are so stylish."

"We have no proper lady's maid to mend our dresses for us." Lydia frowned. "Papa ought to hire one for us. Mattie cannot manage to serve all five of us. Kitty and I are forever neglected."

"Mama tells me I am very clever with my needle." Kitty flushed prettily. "So, I tore one of my gowns to pieces and tried to fit it to the new patterns. I need more fabric and ribbons, maybe some lace, to accomplish all that I intend. My horrid blue gown will be ever so fashionable when I am finished."

"I want a lady's maid." Lydia pouted and crossed her arms over her chest.

Elizabeth looked directly at Kitty. "Remaking the dress is a very clever notion."

Lydia's glare burned the side of Elizabeth's face.

A response would only prolong Lydia's tantrum, so she refused to make eye contact. "I am impressed. Mama declared me hopeless at piecework years ago. I would love to view your designs. Perhaps, if you are willing, you might remake one of my dresses too."

Lydia rolled her eyes and turned aside with an expression that suggested she might cast up her accounts[3] if she heard another word.

Deep, cross voices boomed above stairs, but the words were lost across the distance. A door banged. Feet pounded on the stairs. The front door opened and slammed. They all looked toward the doorway, but no one appeared.

Elizabeth squinted and struggled to make out any scraps of sound that would help her understand what had just happened. Nothing. Her sisters' voices still chattered in the background. She probably should attend to what they were saying, but the strange goings on upstairs had opened up a new hollow in her gut that filled with dread.

"Truly, Lizzy? You would trust me with one of your gowns?" Kitty clasped her hands below her chin. Her smile crinkled the corners of her eyes.

Elizabeth shook her head sharply and blinked. "Certainly. My sprigged muslin cannot be made any worse."

Kitty bounced in her seat. "I shall hurry back from town. Perhaps I might get one of the sleeves finished to show you."

"We were to call upon Maria today." Lydia wrapped her arms around her waist and snorted.

"You go without me." Kitty waved her off. "You complained I was dull company the last time I went with you."

Lydia gagged.

---

[3] Cast up one's accounts: vomit

Elizabeth's eyes widened. Was Lydia frustrated that Kitty did not continue to follow her? Such a little bit of attention, and Kitty was a completely different girl, a much more sensible one. Perhaps Mary was not the only sister she had neglected.

"I shall leave you to make your plans. Come get me when you are ready to show me your work." Elizabeth rose and left.

She plodded upstairs. If she did not get some quiet soon, Bedlam awaited. Too much to consider, too many disturbing thoughts thrown at her too early in the day. She nearly stumbled into Papa as he strode from Mama's room.

He started and grumbled.

"Papa?" She gasped. What turmoil shaded his grey eyes the color of a summer thunderstorm?

"Not now, child. Come talk to me this evening. I need time to think." He nodded sharply and disappeared down the stairs.

She shrugged away the prickling across the back of her shoulders. An odd rumble scuffed at the edges of her consciousness. Mama never cried, but the ragged noises that escaped from beneath the door were bitter sobs.

She approached the door and listened, torn by the knowledge she should not invade Mama's privacy. Perhaps she should get Jane. She always soothed Mama best. Elizabeth edged away from the door. Nevertheless, it inched open, and she peeked in.

The room dripped frills and lace, enough to kill a man. Mama, still in her nightdress, sprawled across her pillow-laden bed and wept.

"Mama?"

She looked up with red-rimmed eyes and blotchy face and rubbed her nose on her sleeves.

Elizabeth slipped inside and shut the door. "Are you ill? Did Aunt Phillips bring bad news? Please tell me what is wrong, and what I may do for your relief." Cold slid over Elizabeth's cheeks and toward her heart.

"Oh, child." Mama pushed herself up, wrapped her arms around her waist, and rocked. "I failed you. I have failed you all."

Elizabeth rubbed Mama's back. What comfort could she offer? She eyed the door. If only Jane, or Papa, or anyone more capable would walk in.

"My sister Phillips came this morning."

Elizabeth bit her lip and tried to smooth the rumpled sheets. "What did she say?"

"Do not tell your sisters." Mama brushed tears from her face with trembling hands.

"Tell them what?" Elizabeth gritted her teeth. At her best, Mama rarely gave a clear answer.

"The Carvers..." Mama's breath hitched, and she swallowed several sobs. "The things that man said about...our friends and neighbors...and my girls."

"Those are just words, empty words. No one gives a curmudgeon like him any credit. Do not fear."

"He said his sisters were harmed by their acquaintances in Meryton. He left town to protect them."

"My sisters are not at fault."

Quicker than Elizabeth thought possible, Mama grabbed her shoulders and shook her hard. "We are ruined. Everyone in town has heard by now. Your sisters' indelicate behavior drove the Carvers away. Aunt Phillips told me not to worry. Since he condemned nearly all of the young ladies in Meryton, it would not reflect upon you girls at all."

"Aunt Phillips is right. You should listen to her."

"No! She has no daughters and does not understand."

"Understand what?" Elizabeth tried to pull away.

"Lydia is so popular. She is a fashion leader who will bear the blame for it all. And all of you with her."

"Papa says not to fear, Mr. Carver's complaints mean nothing—"

Mama shook her harder. Her fingers dug painfully into Elizabeth's upper arms. "Jane is so beautiful, yet Mr. Carver deserted her. The whole town will be saying so by now..." She fell into her pillow, crying hysterically. "No gentleman will ever look at Jane again, nor at any of the rest of you. My dearest Lydia has already been scorned—"

"What do you mean?" Elizabeth swallowed hard against a bitter lump at the back of her throat.

"Do you not recall how Mrs. Smith, Mrs. Long and Mrs. Bond have not been home to any of you girls?"

So, that was who Mary had been talking about.

"Hattie Smith let it slip during tea at the Phillips's that her mother told her not to take tea if the Bennet sisters were present. She has been forbidden to keep company with you any longer. How many others will follow suit? We are ruined. This is too much. Get me my salts."

Elizabeth handed her the broken vinaigrette from the bedside table.

She waved it beneath her nose and revived a moment. Fresh tears spilled down her cheeks as she fingered the damaged chain. "The chatelaine broke when I last visited. I will never be able to show my face in town again. No one will ever receive us again."

Elizabeth's mind whirled. The Smiths, Longs and Bonds, all among the highest standing families in Hertfordshire, had not been home to her either. She and her sisters had truly been cut from society. The walls wavered around her.

Mama continued to speak. But blood roared in her ears and drowned out the words.

"It is my fault. They were right. I could not teach my daughters to be ladies. I should have let them…" Mama turned away and fell into her pillow.

Elizabeth clutched the rumpled sheets in tense fingers. Even if Mama were to blame, she and Jane had done little to check their sisters either. They, too, were responsible for their family's disgrace. The room spun, and she pulled against the sheets to remain upright.

"Leave me now, Lizzy. I have no wish for company." The pillow muffled Mama's command. "Tell your sisters I am not to be disturbed, and tell Hill to allow none of the other servants up, only her." She pulled the counterpane over her head.

Elizabeth watched for three long breaths. "Yes, Mama." She shut the door and gulped in the cool, clear air of the corridor. A scream clawed through her throat. Clenched teeth halted it. What good would it do? No one, nothing could relieve her distress. Papa did not wish to be disturbed now, and Jane—this would be too much for even calm, steady, serene Jane.

"Excuse me, Miss Elizabeth." Hill's gravelly voice startled her. "The post just come with a letter for you."

"Thank you, Hill." Elizabeth accepted the missive. Did Hill notice how her hand shook? "My mother feels very poorly. She asked not to be disturbed and that you alone attend her."

Hill's eyes widened, and her weathered face blanched. "Did she ask to keep all company away?"

"Yes."

"Oh, Miss." Hill's hand flew to her mouth and a wisp of grey hair fell across her forehead. "This is bad, very bad indeed." She glanced up at Elizabeth. "This happened once before, years ago, dontcha know?"

Elizabeth shook her head slowly, her forehead creased tightly.

"You were a wee little thing, still in the nursery. Miss Lydia were just walking, I think. Your mother had a terrible fallin' out with her eldest sister's husband. She had a powerful shock…"

"Uncle Phillips?"

"No, Miss." Hill worried the frayed edge of her apron. "She has another sister. Mrs. Rawls, her name was. It were Mr. Rawls who she had that terrible to-do with, in the parlor no less. The Rawlses, they wanted to take you girls to raise you. They didn't believe the mistress were able to do it proper-like. In the middle of it, he tripped on the carpet and fell. He hit his head on a fire iron and out and died."

Elizabeth gasped and pressed her fist to her lips.

"'Tis true. Mrs. Rawls, she came to pieces, dontcha know. Said it were the mistress's fault her husband died, and the mistress would pay for her wickedness. You girls would be hoydens and strumpets all."

"I never knew."

"It were many years ago. Me and the butler are the only ones still here from those days. We never speak of it so as not to upset the mistress. I should wonder she don't keep fearing about bringin' you young ladies up right, even now."

Had she stepped into the pages of a gothic novel? Secret deaths, relatives threatening to take children, social ruin—when had her life come to this? Elizabeth slumped against the wall.

"The mistress kept to her rooms above stairs for months until we feared for her life. She blamed herself for Mr. Rawls's death and feared Mrs. Rawls's curse.

Thems were dark days at Longbourn." Hill wrung her apron in her hands.

"Perhaps you should check on Mama now. You understand what she needs." A curse as well? If this interview did not end soon, she feared she would run, screaming, from the house.

"I will. Do not fear. I cared for her then, and I will see her through this." Hill glanced down at Elizabeth's hems. "Oh, and do be sure to give Betsy that dress before the mud dries so we can get it proper clean." Hill frowned the frown she had always cast upon a too-lively little girl, bobbed a quick curtsey and slipped into her mistress's rooms.

Elizabeth exhaled heavily, grateful for the wall's support. Her knees barely held up under the weight of the revelations swirling in her mind. Her muddy skirt slapped against her legs. Charlotte was right. Mama was right. Mr. Carver was right.

She and her sisters might very well be ruined, and she was not yet one and twenty.

CHAPTER 4

Elizabeth scurried to her room and slammed the door. Could this be another nightmare? How she hoped to awaken, as she had that morning, to thunder and lighting and relief that her troubles were little more than a dream. But no such comfort presented itself.

Their friends, those she thought were friends, had cut her from their acquaintance as surely as Carver and without nearly so much consideration. A cold ache seeped into her bones.

The sunny warmth of the window seat beckoned her. She curled against the window casing and wrapped her arms around her knees. The glass burned her cheek, hot as her flush of anger at Carver's harsh words. A sharp corner of the letter poked her through her dress.

Aunt Gardiner. Her fingers trembled. She had written her aunt the day of her conversation with Carver. Aunt Gardiner must have written back the same day her letter arrived. *Dear, dear Aunt.* Her lips curled in a weary smile, and she reached into her pocket.

She rubbed the dainty floral 'G' pressed into the sealing wax. Elizabeth bought her the seal as a Christmas gift six years ago. Now it decorated every letter she sent, a silent reminder of their special bond. She broke the wax and smoothed the missive across her lap. The paper crinkled a warm friendly welcome as she traced the greeting. Aunt Gardiner's voice lilted in her ears.

> My dearest Lizzy,
>
> I must confess, I have read your letter three times now and am no more certain where to begin than I was upon my first perusal. Poor Uncle Gardiner will surely go quite distracted. I have been locked in my study these three hours already.
>
> Certainly, you know I only jest, yet I fear it may be true by the time I am finished. Your questions are not easy to answer.
>
> While it is difficult, be careful not to judge the Carvers too quickly. Remember, he is unsure of his place in society and anxious to protect his family. Though hurtful, his actions were born of the best intentions toward those he must care for. I hope this knowledge helps you forgive him. I know you do not like it, but you must forgive, lest his words and actions continue to torment you.

Elizabeth threw her head back and hit the windowpane. Forgive him? No. Scold him, insult him, inform him of his deficiencies, yes. But not forgive. She caught the inside of her cheek in her teeth and exhaled heavily. He did not deserve forgiveness. He had been horrid and cruel…and right.

> You are aware, of course, that the Good
> Book requires we forgive, whether we want to
> or not. Holding on to bitterness only allows
> your anger toward him to rule. Anger will not
> give you the strength to overcome these trials.

She puffed her cheeks and blew out a deep breath. Leave it to Aunt Gardiner to present her with a compelling reason to forgive. She rolled her eyes to the ceiling and chuckled. Indeed, she would attend to that right away, before luncheon, and in the evening help Sisyphus roll his stone over the top of the mountain.

> Neighbors will gossip. Being the object of
> such talk hurts. I am so sorry, my dear, for I
> know it will be difficult.
> Keep in mind, you do not have to sit idle
> and silently confirm their prattle. Show them
> the Bennet girls are better than they say. Your
> actions during the next few weeks will do much
> to determine whether this gossip quietly fades
> away in preference of other interesting tales, or
> it lingers on.
> Allow Jane and Mary to be your allies
> through these difficulties and together, turn the
> tide. I have faith you girls will be able to restore
> yourselves in society even without resorting to
> good dinners and large parties—though I am

sure my sister Bennet already plans a number of them.

Despite the seriousness of the matter, she fought giggles rising in her chest. Elizabeth was not made for unhappiness. Merriment would not be denied. Softly at first, a deep-bellied chortle brought tears to her eyes.

> The curate of my girlhood parish often reminded us the Good Book says all things will work together for good for those who love Him.[4] It may not seem so today, but someday you shall recall these difficult days and be grateful for everything that has happened.
>
> I am not offering empty encouragement. Over and over, I have seen that what I have gained during the trying times is more than I ever realized in the midst of them.
>
> I look forward to your next letter. I must go, for your uncle's sake.
>
> Your loving aunt,
> MG

Elizabeth refolded her letter and placed it in her writing desk. She shook her skirts and blew a deep breath. Perhaps Aunt Gardiner was right. A few words of gossip need not be the end of respectability. *Dear Aunt Gardiner.* She stood, soaking in the sunbeam, the empty ache melting away.

A soft rap at the door drew her attention. She knew the sound and caught Jane's hand as she walked in.

---

[4] Romans 8:28

Jane turned to her, forehead drawn and brows knit. "Mama would not let me in."

"I know." Elizabeth guided her to sit on the edge of the bed and told her what had happened.

For a full minute, Jane only stared and blinked hard, opened her mouth to speak and shut it again before any words came forth. She wandered to the window and traced the mullions with her left index finger. "Mr. Carver spoke the truth. Our sisters are out of control and influencing others to follow their lead. Lizzy, what are we to do?"

"A letter from Aunt Gardiner came today. She says this is our opportunity to show the neighbors that Carver's judgments are untrue."

Jane pressed her forehead against the glass. "Do you not fear it may be too late? So much has already happened. Every time Lydia presents herself in public, she adds more absurdities to the chatter."

"I know." Elizabeth walked to Jane's side and laid her hand on Jane's back. "Yet, I am convinced doing nothing is worse. I would rather try, even if it is futile, than simply surrender."

"Can we do enough to restore our reputations? If we fail, will that not reinforce everything that has been said?" Jane looked over her shoulder into Elizabeth's face. "Can we afford to make things even worse?"

"I am sure between the five of us...or four... we will be able to accomplish whatever needs to be done. We are resourceful young ladies, after all." Elizabeth's tone carried far greater confidence than she felt. A twinge of guilt tickled her side, but she brushed it away. Now was not the time to indulge the fickle sentiment. "I do not know whether the Bonds, the Smiths, and the Longs will ever admit us again, nor can I say I shall miss their company."

Jane hid her face and snorted.

"Tell me you do not find the Miss Smiths' conversations rather insipid, and you do not dread Miss Long's recitations in Italian." Elizabeth winked.

"I would repine the loss of the Miss Bonds' duets on harp and pianoforte—" Jane's fingers danced along an imaginary keyboard.

"They will not become truly proficient if they do not practice. They should take lessons from Mary —"

Mary's distinct triple knock sounded from the doorway.

They shared a mortified smile and tried to quiet their snickers behind their hands.

"Come in." Elizabeth choked back one last titter.

Mary peeked in, slipped inside and shut the door. "Mama?"

Jane and Elizabeth nodded and returned to sit on the bed. Mary joined them, and they stared at each other for several long moments.

"Aunt Phillips did not keep the gossip from town to herself?" Mary asked.

Elizabeth squinched her eyes shut, wrinkled her nose and told Mary everything she had shared with Jane.

Mary swallowed hard and squared her shoulders. "I suppose we must comfort one another with the balm of sisterly consolation."

"How droll you sound." Jane squeaked in her best impression of Lydia.

"We may all become quaint young ladies yet," Elizabeth winked, "if we are to win back the good opinion of our neighbors."

"You will never be called droll, Lizzy." Mary blinked and raised her eyebrows. "I, on the other hand, am much better suited for that description." She straightened her dress and laced her fingers in her lap.

Elizabeth coughed into her fist to cover her laughter. "Given all the attentions he has paid you of late, I am sure a certain curate does not find that to be so bad a thing."

"Lizzy!" Jane glared.

Mary blushed and traced the pattern on the counterpane. "I hope you are correct."

"I believe him well on his way to liking you very much." Jane smiled and patted Mary's hands.

"Do you?" Mary worried her lower lip in her teeth. "Lydia said—"

Elizabeth groaned. "Pay no mind to her. I am certain Lydia believes she is the only one of us that gentlemen should attend. Although she does not desire to be a clergyman's wife, she is jealous of the attention Mr. Pierce pays you."

"What will he do when word of this reaches him?" Mary bit her knuckle and shrank into herself.

"I am sure he has already heard." Elizabeth frowned and shook her head. "After all, who would be better to share such juicy gossip with than the curate?"

"If he is the man we all expect him to be," Jane interrupted with a sharp glance at Elizabeth, "he will not hold it against you." She squeezed Mary's forearm.

"I hope you are right." Mary blinked rapidly, her eyes shimmering.

"She is. Remember, Jane is an excellent judge of character." Elizabeth smiled broadly, though it left an insincere flavor on her tongue. If she did not have faith all would be well, Mary and Jane would not either. At least her courage always rose in the face of intimidation, a strong point in their favor for sure.

Perhaps in light of Mama's condition, Papa would be more apt to hear her concerns and support their efforts. With him behind them, they would prevail.

·•·ᏠᏨᏬ·•·ᏠᏨᏬ·•·ᏠᏨᏬ·•·ᏠᏨᏬ·•·ᏠᏨᏬ·•·

Elizabeth wandered downstairs for at least the tenth time. Perhaps Papa had left his study. The book room door remained shut. She longed to storm in and demand his attention. Over the years though she had learned the tactic rarely produced the desired results. She had no choice but to wait until he was ready.

On her way upstairs, she knocked Kitty's shawl off the hall table. Kitty was home and likely working on her dress. Now would be a good time to fulfill her promises. She picked up the shawl and tucked it under her arm.

Elizabeth took the stairs two at a time, a habit both Hill and Mama detested—*Walk like a lady!* Ladies took too long in getting to their destination, and her desire for distraction overrode her desire for propriety.

Kitty and Lydia's door stood cracked open, so she peeked inside. The yellow walls held the sunlight, bright and lively as her sisters. Bits of fabric and trim lay scattered about like children's playthings left in disarray.

"Oh my." Elizabeth's gaze bounced from one pile to the next.

Kitty jumped, and several curls shook loose around her face. "Lizzy. When did you come in?"

"Only just now. I am sorry. I should have knocked." She chuckled. "Do you usually keep your room this way?"

"I have been so occupied, I did not even think to tidy up." Kitty laughed and set her work aside.

"Apparently. Does Lydia mind?" She moved a pile of garments from a chair, mindful of the pins stuck throughout, and eased herself down.

"Of course she does." Kitty shrugged. Her lip curled, and her pert nose wrinkled.

Elizabeth lifted her brows, but Kitty ducked away.

"I finished the sleeves on my blue gown." She pulled several pins from the fabric and stuck them into her pincushion with a little more energy than strictly necessary.

"Show me. I will help you dress."

"Really? Are you sure?" Kitty squealed and tossed the pincushion aside.

"Absolutely. Turn around so I can reach your buttons."

Kitty presented a long row of small white buttons. "I should have kept my morning dress on and not bothered going into town."

Elizabeth struggled with a particularly stubborn button. "You did not enjoy your trip? You were so anxious to go at breakfast." The muscles on the back of Kitty's neck knotted under Elizabeth's hands. "What happened?"

Kitty's head dropped, and her shoulders sagged. "Nothing."

Elizabeth undid the last button, then ducked around to peer into Kitty's face. "Your expression is quite telling."

"It does not matter." Kitty rolled her eyes and turned away to change gowns. She offered her back again, revealing an equally long row of tiny blue buttons.

Elizabeth tugged the fabric to line up buttons and holes. "What happened?"

"She did what she always does."

"And what is that?"

"Never mind." Kitty sniffed.

"You did a lovely job covering these buttons, you know. I hate the task myself. It is so tedious I fear I will lose my mind." Elizabeth fastened the final two buttons. "Lydia demanded everyone's attention?" She re-pinned Kitty's loose curls.

"Yes." Kitty peeked over her shoulder, lips parted, eyebrows raised so high they nearly touched the curled fringe on her forehead. "She made a spectacle of herself in the process. I was so embarrassed, Lizzy. I tried not to let her know since that only makes it worse." She hugged herself and scanned the room. "I always followed her lead. Now people gawk at us...at me, especially when I am with her. At first it was fun, a game of sorts, but now...I want...I want people to regard me the way they do you and Jane."

Elizabeth's cheeks burned. She tucked another of Kitty's stray locks into place. "I am sorry. I did not realize Lydia made things so difficult for you. I thought you quite pleased with one another."

"Oh, she is happy enough for me to mend and redo her gowns. Lydia enjoys the attention she receives when she wears them." Kitty plucked the ribbons on her bodice. "She treats me as her lady's maid, not her sister."

Elizabeth ground her teeth. "That will not do. For what it is worth, I give you leave not to touch any of Lydia's things again, at least until she practices a proper attitude toward you."

Kitty' jaw dropped. Elizabeth looked over her shoulder. Had a regiment of officers suddenly appeared behind her?

Mama always favored Lydia. When was the last time anyone took Kitty's side? The guilty knot in Elizabeth's side grew a little larger. "Besides, from now on, you shall be far too busy with Jane, Mary and me for any more of Lydia's projects." The corners of Elizabeth's lips twitched. "Even so, I may still beg your indulgence to work on a dress of mine."

"With you and Mary and Jane?" Kitty blinked rapidly. "Doing what?"

"Visiting tenants, making soap, picking honeysuckle and berries—whatever we find for our hands to do, we shall do it with all our heart. It is high time you joined us in being useful." She laughed at Kitty's bewildered expression. "Now, let me see your gown."

Kitty stepped away and modeled. "I used the pattern from the magazine to alter the sleeves—these are the latest fashion in London. I changed the shape of the neckline and added the lace. Then I trimmed the skirt…"

Elizabeth studied the dress and her sister. What a transformation had occurred in both. The gown resembled a fashion plate, and Kitty, a young lady. "Turn around. Show me the back. Oh, you carried the trim all the way across—"

"So you like it?" Kitty bit her lip.

"Kitty, this is brilliant. Truly, I am impressed. You have excellent taste."

Kitty's cheeks glowed. She twirled, hands clasped below her chin.

Elizabeth blushed. Her approval meant so much? This girl hardly resembled the Kitty of her acquaintance. How could she have been so mistaken?

"I want to trim this old bonnet to match the dress." She pressed a half-done shepherdess cap at Elizabeth. "I took extra fabric from the sleeves to use on the crown."

"Oh, I understand what you want to do. Such a smart way to use scraps." Elizabeth pointed to the piles strewn about. "Show me what else you plan to do."

Kitty dug through a pile to retrieve a simple white gown. "I hope to finish this one for the Assembly in town next month." She held it out.

Elizabeth stroked a delicately embroidered pattern on the skirt. "This is lovely. Did you design this pattern yourself?"

Kitty nodded.

"Will you do the entire skirt in the floral scroll?"

"What do you think?" Kitty lifted the skirt into a sunbeam.

Elizabeth stroked the stitches with her fingertip "The subtlety of the white on white is very pleasing. Perhaps a few in silver or gold might—"

"That would be the thing."

"Just a few of them though. Perhaps a touch of the same along the bodice—"

"Perfect! And add pleated ribbon below—" Kitty held the ribbon against the gown.

"What a wonderful idea."

"Thank you, Lizzy." Kitty threw her arms around Elizabeth. "Lydia's tastes are not refined like yours. Any time I ask her opinion, we only argue. She only cares that I make the necklines lower and the sleeves shorter.

If she thought Mama would approve, I am certain she would ask me to take her skirts all the way up to her knees."

Elizabeth shuddered at the image. "Surely she would not. Not even Lydia—"

Kitty shrugged. "Perhaps not, but I think it a very good thing Mama still insists on approving what we wear. You know that Lydia fights with her all the time about necklines and lace tuckers."

"No, I did not." Elizabeth pinched the bridge of her nose. Did Jane and Mary know?

"She wears them when she leaves the house, but as soon as we are away, she removes the lace and pulls her dress down as low as she can. The officers give her so much more attention when she does. She would rather break her arms than wear that dreaded lace."

Elizabeth's stomach danced a disturbed little jig against her ribs. Memories of bawdy images from the print shop windows suddenly bore Lydia's face, and all the men wore red coats. She dug her nails into her palms. The pain helped her focus.

"I should let you get to work while you have the room to yourself. In the future, if Lydia does not permit you to work when you want, you may use Jane's and my dressing room."

Kitty beamed, eyes glittering.

"As long as you promise not to leave it strewn with piles of work." Elizabeth forced a laugh though the effort nearly broke her ribs.

"Of course not." Kitty blushed. "I only leave things this way because it vexes Lydia so."

Elizabeth slipped into the hall. She never had suspected...so many things: the tension between her two youngest sisters; that Kitty followed Lydia for attention, attention she should have had at home, from her sisters, if no one else; Lydia's deceitful ways away from home. When had all this happened?

A fresh knot of guilt joined its sister under her ribs, pushing bile against the back of her tongue. For all she wanted to blame Carver—or anyone else—she could not escape her own failures. Impatience for Papa's company pulsed in her throat. He would help her sort this out.

· • ᷍ᣟᣟ · • · ᷍ᣟᣟ · • · ᷍ᣟᣟ · • · ᷍ᣟᣟ · • · ᷍ᣟᣟ • ·

After no less than six additional trips down the stairs, an open study door rewarded Elizabeth's tenacity. Her heart fluttered as she approached.

"Come in, Lizzy." His voice, heavy and slow, belied the invitation's welcome. A thinning patch of grey hair showed above the back of his chair. "Come in, my dear, and sit down. Hill provided us tea. Someone may as well partake, lest her feelings be wounded." He waved her in without turning around.

She hesitated at the doorway, searching for signs of what troubled him. A pile of unfamiliar ledgers and papers occupied his desk. Had Uncle Phillips brought those? She sat on the footstool beside him instead of the opposite chair. Her unladylike perch never failed to make him smile. He did not disappoint although the expression held only a shadow of its usual warmth.

She poured one teacup full of water and a second half full. The creaky-squeaky tea caddy complained when she opened it to spoon measures of tea into each cup and again on closing. The sound—or was that tension—raised the hairs on the back of her neck. She glanced at Papa, who peered out the window with a dull stare. Why did he not complain about the squeaky hinges?

Streams of color flowed away from the tea leaves into the hot water, swirling and blending into one another. She chose a lump of sugar with the tongs and set it on a saucer to nip off a corner. The smaller piece went into the half cup followed by three spoons full of cream. She stirred. The spoon clinked against the cup. Perhaps he would take notice.

He turned to her, his eyebrows inched up, and his mouth curled into a wrinkled frown. She winked and stood. Teacup in hand, she ambled to the brandy decanter and added two spoons full. "I know you like your French cream." The spoon clinked again.

"Do take pity on me, Lizzy." He laughed and reached for the cup. "We both know you can make a man a proper cup of tea. You do not need to torture him in the process."

"It got you to smile." She returned to her perch on the footstool and sipped her tea.

He smiled at her, a genuine smile this time that eased the tightness in her chest. The light in his eyes faded with a second sip of tea. "You saw your mother."

"I did."

"Did she say anything to you?"

Elizabeth studied her teacup, admiring the patterns of the leaves swirling in the bottom. "She did. Hill also spoke with me before she went to Mama."

"So you understand, she needs time to recover." He placed his teacup on the table and pushed on the chair arms to stand. He shuffled to his desk and leaned on the stack of worn ledgers. "When your mother and I married, some questioned the ability of a tradesman's daughter to raise you to be the ladies you should be. Those words have haunted her since. Given what Carver supposedly said—"

"Papa, it is not simply rumored. When I called upon the Miss Carvers, after the Netherfield ball, he refused me admittance and—"

A growl rumbled in his throat and cut her off. He clasped his hands behind his back and paced in front of his desk. Two, three, four times he crossed in front of her.

"Papa?"

He drew a shuddering breath. "I am well, child." He gulped in another lungful. "It is a good thing he left the neighborhood."

Elizabeth stared. Papa always laughed at the foibles of his neighbors. He never became angry. She drew a deep breath.

He lifted a hand and shook his head.

This was not the Papa she expected to find. Her expectation of comfort ebbed away. If anything, he seemed to need her support, something she would never deny him even at the cost of her own ease.

"I forbade your Aunt Phillips from visiting your mother until she is ready to leave her rooms again. I will not—"

"You do not believe Aunt Phillips would intentionally—"

"I will not speculate on her motives. She should know better. Your uncle and I have warned her often enough." He leaned across the desk and picked up the pile of journals and a stack of loose papers.

Since Lizzy still occupied the footstool, he placed them on the chair she should have used and pushed it closer to his own seat. She scooted aside to allow him to pass. He dropped into his chair with a soft thud.

"The estate's spring business requires my attention right now, and Hill cannot run the house on her own. I have no alternative but to look to you and Jane to take over for your mother until she is well." He worked his tongue against the roof of his mouth as though to rid himself of an unpalatable taste. "I realize she has done little to prepare you to be mistress of an estate. Nevertheless, I am confident you will rise to the occasion." He smiled, but his eyes were blank and dull.

Run the house? Repairing the family's reputation would be a full time occupation. So would managing

Lydia. How could they do it all? She set her rattling teacup and saucer aside.

He leaned toward her and offered his hand. She grasped it with both of hers. His large hands covered her and gripped them tightly.

She swallowed hard and managed a weak smile. "What needs to be done? I imagine that rather impressive stack of papers and books holds many of the answers?" She slipped a hand from his and plucked the loose papers off the top of the pile.

"Those are your mother's lists of tenant needs." He removed his glasses from his coat pocket and perched them on his nose. "Bring those a little closer." He peered over her shoulder. "Let me see. Yes, one for each family, with clothes for the children, foodstuffs, needed repairs on the houses—"

Elizabeth squinted over the text. "I do not recall Mama ever calling upon the tenants."

"She usually waits until you girls are out of the house. She does not want to burden you with their hardships."

"What are those journals?" She chin pointed at the large stack.

He passed the first book to her. "This is her book of recipes, some of them passed down from her mother and mine. I understand Hill consults it often to instruct the cook and maids. I believe she has a few additional recipes somewhere in the stack of notes to add to it."

Elizabeth leafed through the pages of Mama's careful handwriting. Each loop and swirl revealed a side of Mama she had never known. He pressed another book into her hands.

"This is one of the household ledgers. She records the accounts of the eggs and dairy here." He added another book on the heap, "In this one she keeps the records from each of the shopkeepers with whom she does business."

The pile of books in her lap grew larger still with the addition of the book of menus and guests for each dinner hosted at Longbourn over the last five years and the one detailing the Christmas gifts provided for tenants, cottagers and villagers for ten years at least. "I never imagined Mama so meticulous." She closed the volume and smoothed over the scrolls embossed on its cover.

"Few know. She complains her memory is not good, thus she writes everything down. I think it more the product of her fears she is insufficient to her role as mistress of Longbourn. Either ways, it is to your advantage since nearly all you will need can be found in those books. What is not, Hill can assist you with."

"I never realized." Elizabeth stretched and rubbed the back of her neck. "No wonder great men employ stewards and secretaries to help them in their work."

"Your mother has done an admirable job, and I am certain you and Jane will as well."

"I appreciate your confidence, Papa, but I am not sure I share it." Her eyebrows rose and fell.

He sighed heavily. "If there were any other way—"

"No, Papa, please do not feel guilty. I am glad for the opportunity to learn. I only wish the circumstances were different."

"We all do." He chewed his upper lip and stared at the ceiling, blinking hard.

"I shall go and begin my studies." She gathered the books and papers and trudged upstairs. Her heart weighed as much as the ledgers in her arms. How could she bear even one more burden? Her eyes prickled. She blinked away the burn. Aunt Gardiner said she was not alone though. Jane and Mary would be with her and perhaps now Kitty too. She drew a deep breath. A cord of many strands would not easily break.[5]

---

[5] Ecclesiastes 4:12

CHAPTER 5

Elizabeth rubbed her eyes and shut the cover of Mama's book of recipes and household management instructions. Her grandmothers' and mother's voices whispered in her ears. Women she had often dismissed as trivial, and even silly, now gave her decades of wisdom she never knew existed. Though she would probably always prefer Plato and Aristotle, this tome forced her to confront an uncomfortable truth: she never understood the depths of her own ignorance. Would she ever have something worthy to add to these books?

She scrubbed her face with her hands. If only she could get Lydia to see the importance of their efforts and join the rest of them. At least she had to try.

First, she needed sleep. The problem of Lydia would wait until morning.

After her near-dawn walk, Elizabeth returned to Mama's books. She listened for activity from her sisters' rooms and invited them in to join her as they rose. Naturally, Lydia slept the latest.

"Do sit down already. Must you wear a hole in the carpet?" Elizabeth drummed her fingers against the bedpost.

"Mr. Carver is such a cod's head." Lydia huffed and stomped. She dropped to the window seat and pounded the cushion.

"Really, Lydia,—" Jane smoothed the bedcovers and squirmed.

Lydia wrapped her arms across her chest and turned away.

Elizabeth dug her nails into her palms. As a child, Lydia would dress up in Mama's old gowns and throw tantrums because her sisters did not obey her directions. Twelve years later, nothing had changed.

"What is not proper is all the fuss and bother for that old fumbler." Lydia peeked over her shoulder and huddled back into the window.

Mary frowned from her perch on the wooden chair in the corner. "How can you call our neighbors cutting us merely fuss and bother?" She crossed her legs and bobbed her foot.

"None of them that cut us are worth the acquaintance." Lydia whipped around and sneered.

"Fudge! And you know it." Kitty jumped to her feet and nearly bounced Jane and Elizabeth off the bed.

"The Smiths, the Longs and the Bonds are good families. We have all been friends for—"

"Who needs them? The officers are in Meryton." Lydia tucked her knees under her chin. "They are ever so much more entertaining than the likes of the Miss Whom-ever-they-may-be's."

"For as long as the regiment remains." Kitty stomped to the window seat. "Did you forget, the regiment will move away to Brighton soon enough, and all we will be left with are the Miss Whom-ever's you think unworthy of your time now?"

Lydia waved her down. "I shall have a husband by then, and I am sure I will not care."

"How do you mean to get a husband when you chase all the men in town away?" Kitty snorted.

"Mr. Carver is a cow-handed[6] conscience keeper[7] and not worth having. I believe I did Jane a favor in removing him from her presence." Lydia gawked at Jane. "You did not like him, did you?"

"It does not matter if I did or not." Jane shook her head and squeezed her temples. "Your behavior has brought judgment upon all of us, and now Mama keeps to her rooms." Tight little lines formed beside her mouth.

"Mama always complains of her nervous spasms. This is no different. She will be well in a day or two,

---

[6] Cow-handed: awkward
[7] **Conscience keeper:** A superior, who by his influence makes his dependents act as he pleases.

and all will be forgotten." Lydia flicked the notion aside.

"Papa thinks not." Elizabeth stalked to the dressing table and scooped up Mama's journals. "He said until Mama recovers, which he expects shall be *months*, we will be in charge of the household." She pressed books at each of them.

"We?" Lydia ducked her chin and shuddered. "I hardly think he said that. I am certain he said *you* should handle all this since you are the cleverest of us all."

Elizabeth cringed. Lydia made clever sound like a moral failure.

"I am no servant. I shall do nothing of the kind." Lydia flipped through the leather bound volume and slammed it shut.

"Lydia! Consider your duty." Mary's bouncing foot hit the floor loudly.

"Mama never lifts a finger. Why should I?" Lydia stood and dusted off her skirts.

Elizabeth ground her teeth until they squeaked. Pain shot through her jaw. Jane laid a hand on her arm. Did Jane guess she longed to shake Lydia?

"You are never home to notice. You are always off gossiping." Kitty's shoulders bobbed in time with her words.

"Who do you believe handles those responsibilities?" Elizabeth pushed herself up from the bed and took a small step nearer Lydia.

"I neither know nor care. I will have servants to do such things for me, and I will have them sooner than all of you. I am about the business of catching a husband, not dirtying my hands with eggs and cows and tenants." She threw the ledger at Elizabeth. "You take this. I am going to Maria's. We will have tea with Mrs. Forster this afternoon." She flounced her skirt and left.

They all stared in her wake.

"Well," Elizabeth placed the ledger on the bed, "I suppose that could have gone better though I am not entirely surprised."

"Are you surprised at all?" Kitty rolled her eyes and took Lydia's place in the window seat.

"No, I am not," Mary said.

"What are we to do if she will not listen?" Jane hunched over her lap.

"We will do what Aunt Gardiner said. We will show everyone the Bennet girls are women of worth and virtue." Elizabeth squared her shoulders and lifted her chin. Her heart drummed a loud beat against her ribs, as loud as Mary's stomach grumble across the room.

"It is sound advice." Mary sighed and perched her elbows on her knees. "Where do we begin?"

"With breakfast." Jane's head came up sharply, and she hauled herself to her feet. "We can take this conversation downstairs and continue over kippers and scones. I cannot consider heavy issues whilst I am hungry." She opened the door and shooed Mary and Kitty out.

Elizabeth collected the journals and stopped at the door. "You are not hungry."

"No, I am not." Jane looked down. "I just needed a moment to collect myself."

"We can do this, Jane." She took her sister's hand.

"It is Lyddie." Jane shrugged. "Mrs. Forster is such a young woman, newly married. I wonder if she is fitting company for our sister."

"Lydia is only going for tea. I expect little harm from only an afternoon." Elizabeth nodded, lips pressed tight.

"I hope so. Lydia has a talent for the ridiculous, though." Jane leaned her cheek against the doorjamb. "This feels so unreal. I keep hoping I will wake up—"

"I know, but ignoring this will not improve matters. We must do whatever we are able to do. Mary would say 'Each should carry their own load—'"[8]

"Or 'Whatever your hand finds to do, do it with all your heart.'"[9] Jane's smile returned. "We should not tease her for her ability to quote the Good Book."

Elizabeth pulled her through the doorway and toward the stairs. "How else might we tease her? She is so—"

"Dull?"

"No."

"Serious?" Jane paused at the top of the stairs.

"Yes, serious. She is difficult to make sport of."

"And you cannot ignore the challenge." Jane smirked and hurried down the stairs.

---

[8] Galatians 6:5
[9] Ecclesiastes 9:10

Of all her sisters', Jane's disquiet disturbed her the most. The others were easily unsettled while only the greatest upset would move Jane from her usual serenity.

Elizabeth joined her sisters in the morning room, one of her favorite rooms at Longbourn. Snug and sunny, with pieces from her grandmothers Bennet and Gardiner along the walls, warmth and welcome reigned. She served her plate, and they ate in companionable silence for a few minutes.

"So, where shall we begin today?" Elizabeth passed out Mama's ledgers.

Papers and pages rustled, punctuated by sighs and other small sounds of dismay. Kitty and Mary grinned and swapped books. Jane cocked her head at Elizabeth and offered a similar exchange. Journals changed hands several more times.

"Well," Jane folded her arms across her chest, "I prefer to leave the household accounts to you, Lizzy. I would rather manage Mama's social correspondence. She planned two small dinners in the next month. I believe we should go ahead and host them. With Mama's notes and Hill's assistance, I believe we can do a credible job conducting them ourselves."

"I can only imagine the gossip if we canceled them." Mary shifted several loose sheets of paper on the table.

"Mama loves company so. She might even come down and join us while we have guests." Kitty leaned across the table to read the stack of notes in front of Jane.

"Even if she does not, I am certain it would ease her heart knowing our neighbors were not disappointed," Elizabeth said.

"If none of you mind," Mary scanned their faces, "I should like to visit the tenants and attend to their needs. Several of the children have taken colds, and I have some teas to bring them."

"You are well suited for the task." Elizabeth laughed softly. "I fear I am better fitted to arguing with merchants and commanding servants."

"So you will supervise them all?" Kitty rifled the pages of the nearest journal.

"I suppose so. What would you prefer to do?"

"Would you think me odd if I want take over the eggs and milk?"

"I do think you very odd, but I am most happy the task will fall to someone other than me." Elizabeth laughed heartily and pushed away from the table. "Well, off with you to the pasture and eves[10]." She gathered papers and ledgers from the table. "I shall lock myself away in the pantry to study if you will excuse me."

Elizabeth retreated to the housekeeper's room off the kitchen and poured over Mama's recipes and lists until dinnertime.

Mr. Bennet did not join them for dinner. A short note informed them he would eat with the Phillipses. So, Lydia dominated the dinner table conversation with details of her afternoon spent at Mrs. Forster's and the

---

[10] Eves: poultry roosts

invitation to join her again the next day. Lydia acted surprised when her sisters quickly retired from the dining room and retreated upstairs. She followed, complaining loudly of how jealous they must be that Mrs. Forster liked her best of all.

·•·❧❦·•·❧❦·•·❧❦·•·❧❦·•·❧❦·•·

The next morning, while her younger sisters ate breakfast, Lizzy stood shoulder to shoulder with Hill, hunched over Mama's ledger in the tiny housekeeper's room. The limited light from the narrow window made it difficult to stand without casting shadows on the pages.

"I need your assistance." Elizabeth opened the ledger.

"Yes, Miss." Hill bobbed in a small curtsy that nearly knocked the book off the table. She clasped her hands so tightly, her knuckles turned white.

Lizzy pointed to several specific entries. "I noticed we have purchased sugar more often in the last six months. I examined the menus, and I do not understand why we should be running out of sugar so much faster now."

Hill's eyes grew wide and she scratched her head. "I cannot for the life of me think why, Miss. My girls don't steal. I watches them myself—"

"No, no, I do not accuse the staff." Elizabeth lifted an open hand. "Do you check the weight of the items the merchants send?"

"Oh, yes, I do. Mr. Sterling's parcels are always correct, dontcha know." Hill wrung her apron. "I can show you the scales." She beckoned Elizabeth to the corner of the kitchen, near the back door. "The girls put the packages on the table next to my scale. Nothing moves until I do the weighing. None of them read good, so I do it all meself."

Elizabeth tested the scale against the calibrating weights. "Everything appears in order." She pressed her lips into a thoughtful frown. "How odd. What is this?" She led Hill to a small pile of stones on the floor in the far corner of the pantry.

"I cannot imagine what thems is doing in my kitchen. Betsy." Hill stepped into the kitchen proper. "Betsy."

"Yes, ma'am." A nervous bird of a woman dashed in and skidded to a stop before Hill.

"Why are them rocks in my pantry?" Hill pointed a quivering finger.

"I'm sorry, ma'am. I usually remember to take them out. I forgot." Betsy bobbed awkwardly and scurried to the pile. She scooped them into her apron.

"Take them out? How do they get in?" Hill tapped a staccato beat with her foot against the stone floor.

"The sugar. I find them in the bags of sugar. Now, I sieve them before I bring it to Cook. She wanted to lace my jacket[11] good the first day I brung her the sugar with them rocks in." Betsy glanced up, adding the last of the

---

[11] Lace my jacket: to beat me soundly

pebbles to her apron. She clambered to her feet. "Cook was in a hurry for the sugar this time, and I dropped 'em. I meant to come clean 'em up, I did."

"And you did not tell me?" Hill pulled herself up taller and scowled.

"What was to tell?" Betsy's shoulders twitched.

"Thank you, Betsy." Elizabeth schooled her features into her best mistress-of-the-manor expression. "In the future, Mrs. Hill will check the contents of all the parcels. You may return to your duties."

"Yes, ma'am." Betsy dipped a curtsey and scampered away so quickly she stumbled twice before she reached the safety of the back door.

Lizzy smiled wryly. "Now we know why the sugar has been running out so fast."

"I am sorry, Miss. I had no idea. If that girl would have told me…"

"It is all right, Hill. She clearly did not know better. Do not punish her for this." Elizabeth chewed her lower lip. "The question is, what to do now?"

"I have an idea, if I may, Miss." Hill's lips pulled back in a gap-toothed grin. She rubbed her hands together. "I will tell our girls of Mr. Sterling's cheating ways and send them on errands to the other houses in the neighborhood. In a day or so, everyone will know."

"Very fitting." Elizabeth chuckled and nodded. "Of course, we will take our patronage to Mr. Nash now."

"I do believe many in town will soon agree, dontcha know. That will take care of him soon enough."

"I am sure you are correct. Still, Mr. Sterling needs to be told directly we will no longer order from him. I will go into town and tell him."

"Beggin' your pardon, Miss, you might want to consult the Master first. Thems merchants get awfully hot, and they ain't gentlemen, if you know what I mean."

"Thank you for your concern, Hill. I am certain I can manage."

"Yes, Miss, if you are sure—"

"I am. I will inform you of the new orders when I return."

··•❧❦··•❧❦··•❧❦··•❧❦··•❧❦··

Elizabeth discovered her sisters still in the morning room. They listened to Lydia recount her adventures at Mrs. Forster's house. The rolled eyes and slack-jawed expressions left no doubt, Lydia alone found pleasure in the accounts. She fell into her chair, and the ledger landed on the table with a glass-rattling thud.

Jane poured her a cup of tea. "We missed you at breakfast."

"La, do not be a goose. We hardly noticed she was gone." Lydia laughed but stopped abruptly to throw a sour look at Mary. "We would have had a perfectly merry time without your sermonizing."

"I merely suggested you should devote yourself to what needs be done at home rather than—"

"Go spend the day with Mrs. Forster," Lydia sing-songed, bouncing her shoulders in time. "Just because you are jealous of me does not mean you should take away all my fun." She pushed away from the table. "See if I tell any of you the gossip I shall hear whilst I am there." She screwed up her face and stuck out her tongue.

Kitty turned away and grimaced as Lydia sashayed through the door.

"It seems I missed quite the conversation." Elizabeth braced her elbows on the table.

"At least Colonel Forster is a sensible man. Men of sense do not want silly wives," Mary said. "I am sure he will watch over both of them."

"I hope you are right." Elizabeth raised her head. "I must go into town. Do any of you—"

"Yes." All three exclaimed in unison, then looked at each other and tittered.

"I need to go to the library," Mary said.

"And visit the chandler[12] and the vintner." Jane produced a list from her pocket. She squinted as she read. "The apothecary, too. Hill needs ingredients for a tea for Mama."

"And I need fabric…I am going to help Mary sew baby dresses." Kitty beamed at Mary.

"Mrs. Anderson is close to her confinement. This will be her sixth, and all her baby clothes are quite worn out," Mary added.

---

[12] Chandler: candle seller, often also sold tea

"Too bad Lydia hurried off. We all might have gone into town together." Kitty snorted.

Jane sighed. "I can be ready in a quarter of an hour."

"A quarter hour then." Elizabeth rose, and her sisters followed.

·•·❧❧·•·❧❧·•·❧❧·•·❧❧·•·❧❧·•·

Elizabeth raced up the front steps and landed against the door, hands outstretched. "First!" She laughed and looked over her shoulder.

Her sisters, backlit by the sunset, ran toward her, panting and laughing.

"Not fair!" Kitty jumped the last two steps and huffed beside her. "You got a head start."

"You should pay better attention." Elizabeth grinned and shoved unruly locks behind her ears. "Hurry up. Jane! Mary! Do not be such gadabouts."

"Not all of us walk as you do, Lizzy. Have mercy." Jane dragged up the steps, leaning heavily on Mary's arm.

"That was not a walk. We ran the last mile at least." Mary pushed the door open.

Papa pulled the door at the same time and threw Mary off balance. She stumbled and fell into him. He caught her with a startled grunt and righted her to her feet. "What kept you so long? You know better than to stay out near nightfall."

"I am sorry, Papa." Elizabeth kissed his cheek and unbuttoned her pelisse. "We were busy. The time got away from us."

He glared at her, but his expression soon softened. "I am glad you are come home. Let me help you with your baskets."

Mary and Jane handed him their burdens.

"You went to the library?" He set the baskets on the hall table and peeked inside. "*Mrs. Chapone's Letters to the Improvement of the Mind*? Mrs. Rundell's *A New System of Domestic Cookery*? *A Household of Economy*? *A Lady's Manual of Household Accounts*?" He glanced at his daughters who all shrugged and he opened the other basket. "*Herbs of England and Recipes for the use Thereof*? *The Care and Maintenance of Poultry*? *A Gentlewoman's Guide to Dairy*?"

"Papa?" Jane laid a hand on his shoulder.

"Girls…" His voice cracked and he blinked rapidly. He opened his arms and drew all four of them into his embrace at once. "It is time for dinner. Tell me of your trip while we eat."

They set aside the rest of their packages and followed him.

"It is about time you came for dinner." Lydia stomped into the dining room. "I am so hungry. Papa said we could not eat until you returned." She fell gracelessly into her chair and hugged her belly. "It was most thoughtless of you to be so late."

Elizabeth snuck a peep at Jane who closed her eyes and shook her head. They seated themselves around the table. Mr. Bennet said a brief grace and tucked his napkin into his collar.

"Pass the potatoes, Mary. Do not hog them so." Lydia stretched across Kitty for the dish.

"Lyddie," Jane whispered, "do not be unkind."

Lydia scowled. "Mary hogs her favorite dishes and keeps them out of reach for the rest of us."

Mary flushed bright red and clamped her jaws shut tightly. She passed three more dishes to Kitty to give to Lydia. "Is there something else you would care for?"

Elizabeth cringed. Mary must be very tired. She rarely indulged in sarcasm.

Lydia arranged the platters within her reach and helped herself from them all. "You will be sorry you did not get to visit Mrs. Forster today."

"I do not think we missed anything at all," Kitty said to her plate. "We had a perfectly lovely time in town."

"Oh, really, who did you see?" Lydia cocked her head and lifted her brows.

"The librarian, the linen draper—"

"No one of any significance, whereas, I saw three lieutenants and a major—"

"Officers again," Mary muttered under her breath.

"Not only officers, though they were by far the most entertaining folk. I saw Mrs. Lawton, too. Guess what she told me."

"We do not need gossip." Jane smoothed the napkin in her lap. "It is something best for all of us to avoid. Would it not be better to—"

"No! I will tell my story." Lydia plunked her glass down loud enough to rattle Kitty's plate.

"You are always talking." Kitty crossed her arms over her chest.

"I am not. No one gets the chance with you in the room." Lydia stuck her tongue out at Kitty.

Jane pinched the bridge of her nose.

"Since you must tell it, speak already, Lydia," Mr. Bennet did not look up from his mutton. "We will get no peace until you do."

Lydia grinned. She wore a triumphant-over-her-sisters smirk that turned Elizabeth's stomach. Elizabeth pushed her plate away.

"Well, I took tea with Mrs. Forster today when who should come to call but Aunt Phillips and Mrs. Lawton and her daughter. And she, I mean Emily, not Mrs. Lawton, wore the most beautiful new lace trim—"

"No! No lace. I beg of you." Mr. Bennet landed his hands heavily on the table. "If I must hear this, there is to be no talk of lace."

Lydia huffed. "Well, Mrs. Lawton told us Mr. Carver's upstairs maid told her scullery maid who told her lady's maid the reason they removed so suddenly from Netherfield."

Elizabeth grimaced and bit her lip so hard she tasted blood.

"She said he found the company in Meryton savage." Lydia giggled. "Imagine that, savage."

Jane flicked her eyes from Elizabeth to Mary and Papa.

"She also said he objected to the regiment and the town crawling with officers." Lydia laughed. "Who could object to officers?"

"If you consider how little we know—" Mary wrung her napkin.

"Nor did the officers' wives impress him." Lydia added with a flourish. "How could he find fault with Mrs. Forster? She used to join us when we called upon his sisters—"

"That is quite enough, Lydia." Mr. Bennet cleared his throat.

Elizabeth's head snapped up. That sound meant Papa had little patience left. She peeked at clueless Lydia, unaware of the danger she courted.

"Oh, Papa, you do not want to be a bore, do you? Let me finish—"

"Excuse me?" The glasses rang, echoing his voice. He leaned toward her, jaw clenched. "You will do me the courtesy of obedience. If you wish to be permitted to visit Mrs. Forster next week, you will be most circumspect with what you choose to say next."

Lydia's cheeks flushed, and her chin quivered. She jumped up to dash away from the table.

"Perhaps now we might enjoy sensible conversation," he muttered and returned to his plate. The deep lines in his forehead became deeper as he sawed his meat.

Kitty shook her head and shrank away. Mary huddled into her chair. Jane stared at the window.

Elizabeth's courage failed her too when he showed this side of himself. She put a small piece of mutton in her mouth. The succulent meat became tasteless and too dry to swallow. "Lydia received an invitation from Mrs. Forster?" She hid behind her water glass and drank deeply to wash down the meat lodged in her tight throat.

He finished chewing his bite and carefully placed his utensils on his plate. The lines around his mouth eased as he looked up at his daughters. "Forgive my outburst, girls. As to your question, Mrs. Forster invited Lydia to stay until the regiment leaves for Brighton."

"You gave her leave to do so?" Jane asked.

"Yes." He held up his hand. "Your thoughts are clear upon your faces, Lizzy, Mary. I will not entertain discussion on this point."

Mary withered in her chair. Jane dropped her gaze to the table. Kitty squirmed and rolled the tablecloth between her fingers. Elizabeth's breath hitched, and she bit her tongue.

"I must be away on important business, and I need to leave soon. You will all have enough on your plate without reining in Lydia as well. Colonel Forster curbs an entire regiment. I think he can maintain a fifteen-year-old girl well enough."

Elizabeth opened her mouth to protest.

He leaned toward her, brows pulled down low.

She closed her mouth and pressed her fist to her lips.

"Where are you going, Papa?" Jane whispered.

"Kent, with your Uncle Phillips."

"May I ask, what is your business in Kent?" Elizabeth said through her hand.

"No, you may not."

Her ears stung as though boxed, and her eyes burned. She quickly turned aside to shield her face with her napkin and blinked rapidly.

His posture softened. "We will talk on my return."

"Yes, Papa," she murmured, not looking at him.

He sighed and tried to catch her eye.

She refused.

He returned to his plate for several bites. "So, tell me of your trip to town. You did more than visit the library." His voice no longer carried a sharp edge.

"We accomplished many errands today," Jane said and nudged Elizabeth's foot under the table. "We spoke to the merchants..."

"To learn their wares..." Kitty added.

"And their prices." Mary scooped potatoes onto her plate.

"Oh, Papa." Jane tittered. "You should have seen Lizzy. She had the two dry goods merchants ready to come to blows in the middle of the street."

He choked on his food and sputtered, "Well, since neither has come to my door, I know they were not fighting for her hand." He swiped his eyes with his napkin.

Elizabeth gasped while the others laughed. "Papa, how could you? I was not flirting with the merchants. I am not—"

"Oh, no, my dear. I would never accuse you of flirting, much to your poor mother's dismay." He winked. "I seem to recall several memorable lectures aimed at encouraging you to develop that skill, none of which were well received."

Elizabeth rolled her eyes and shook her head. Her sisters laughed harder. She wanted to join in, but her voice caught in her throat in a suffocating mass.

"So, go on." He beckoned words from Jane, but leaned toward Elizabeth.

She focused on her folded hands.

"Lizzy went to Mr. Sterling's shop to inquire after the cost of sugar, tea and coffee," Mary said.

Elizabeth looked up.

"He would not give her an answer. Can you believe that?" Kitty lowered her voice and rounded her shoulders in a rough imitation of the shopkeeper. " 'Hill has patronized my shop for many years. She is a competent and trustworthy woman. Do not question her judgment now.' "

"Oh, your face, Lizzy." Jane snickered through pressed lips. "You were the picture of righteous outrage. I expected he would fall dead just from the way you glowered at him."

"She did not deign to speak to him further." Mary guffawed and reached for a roll.

"She spun on her heel and stalked out of the shop, leaving us all to scurry after her like little ducklings." Kitty stepped her fingers lightly across the table.

"And we all fell in behind her." Jane covered her mouth and laughed. "We followed mama-duck directly across the street to talk to Mr. Nash."

"Who quickly gave me the answers I requested, I might add." Elizabeth met Papa's gaze. "In fact, he offered an excellent price if we would switch our patronage to his shop."

Papa chewed his thumbnail and nodded.

"At just that moment, Mr. Sterling stormed in, declaring Lizzy had led us away too soon. He meant no offense, rather a compliment to the staff of Longbourn," Jane said. "Lizzy would have none of it. She dismissed him like an unwanted suitor, refusing to hear him at all."

"So he became angry—" Mary began.

"—and they threw him out—" Kitty interrupted.

"—so he yelled from the street—"

"—and the shop assistant followed him to try and silence him—"

"—the young man could not—"

"—so his father followed him." Mary and Kitty gasped and laughed as they finished each other's sentences.

Lizzy looked at the ceiling and frowned. The whole affair had not been nearly so sensational. Had it? "It was not so entertaining as that, Papa. Mr. Nash tried to calm Mr. Sterling—"

"They almost came to blows." Kitty blurted. "Mr. Sterling accused Mr. Nash of trying to steal our patronage from his shop, and Mr. Nash shouted no law forbade competition. Then Mr. Sterling struck—"

"No, he pushed Mr. Nash. Mr. Sterling did not hit him." Mary dabbed her face with her napkin. "Then the regiment paraded through and effectively broke off their…interaction."

"Indeed." Papa cupped his chin and tapped his lips with his index finger. The creases on his forehead deepened.

"The price she negotiated on our tea, coffee, and sugar for the next month will please you very much." Jane winked.

He gazed directly at Elizabeth, brows pulled together in a single shaggy awning over his narrowed eyes. "I appreciate your efforts. However, in the future, I will handle disputes with the merchants."

Elizabeth ducked her head, her cheeks burned, neck burned, ears burned, even her scalp prickled. What a spectacle she had caused. If only she could crawl under the table and hide. She squeezed her eyes shut. Her lungs screamed for breath, but her pinched throat barely cooperated.

The truth hung in the air.

Her behavior was no better than Lydia's.

"When will you leave, Papa?" Jane asked.

"I will be here to escort you to church tomorrow. On Monday, I will leave with my brother Phillips."

"So quickly?" Mary gasped.

"Yes." He sighed heavily. "Now, no long faces. We should enjoy this delightful pie Cook has offered us."

He served the pastry and pushed a plate at Elizabeth. "Tell me what happened after the regiment passed?"

The conversation swirled around her, but Elizabeth barely heard. The look in Papa's eyes had rattled her very core. He almost never used that tone with her. A slap to the face would have been less painful. Memories of the people on the streets of Meryton, witnesses to the frightful display between Nash, Sterling and herself, flashed in her mind, each one a picture of judgment and condemnation. Her chest burned with each lungful. What would their neighbors say about them now?

·•·‹ఞ·•·‹ఞ·•·‹ఞ·•·‹ఞ·•·

Elizabeth sat curled in the window seat and tried to make herself as small as possible. Decorum had not permitted her to hide under the dining table. But in the solitude of her room, she found refuge from the looks and the questions, the hollow anecdotes and efforts to improve her frame of mind. Luckily, she had eaten little. Casting up her accounts would have drawn more attention.

What a rare opportunity she had to examine her hubris. Oh, her intentions—the salvation of her family's good name—earned the title "noble", little good that it did. She had been so certain in her mission, she ignored the advice, wisdom, and protection of those around her. Hill cautioned her before she left. Mary and Jane added their concerns. In her pride and conceit, she would not deign to listen.

Tears vexed her with their stubborn refusal to gather in sufficient quantities for a soul-cleansing cry. She snorted at the irony; she hated to cry.

Elizabeth pulled her shawl around her shoulders. An owl hooted in the distance. Papa's snores filtered in, reminders of his anger and disappointment. A teardrop leaked. Just one. She chuckled. One foolish tear to capture the depth of her sorrow. She could not even do that right.

Arms wrapped about her knees, she picked at the frayed hem on the sleeve of her nightdress. Maybe Kitty—

The door whispered a squeak to a soft rustle of fabric. Bare feet padded toward her.

"Are you well?" Jane sat beside her.

Elizabeth rested her forehead on her knees. "I thought Aunt Gardiner right. We—I—might be able to redeem the Bennet name."

"You doubt now?" Silvery moonbeams haloed Jane in an ethereal glow.

Elizabeth balanced her chin on her knees and huffed. "You do not? After what happened in town today—"

"You mean Mr. Sterling and Mr. Nash?" Jane cocked her head and leaned close.

"What else?" Elizabeth unfurled and slid off the window seat. She paced in the moonlight, her shadow obscured Jane's face as she passed. "You heard Mary's and Kitty's descriptions. What a disgraceful exhibition. How many stood around to gape at the show?"

"People gawk all the time."

"Not at…at me."

"You cannot compare yourself to Lydia—"

"Why not? I created a public spectacle that nearly resulted in fisticuffs—"

"Stop!" Jane grabbed her hand and forced her to stand still. "You know none of that came from flirting or showing off. You tried to address a wrong, one perpetrated, do not forget, upon the whole of Meryton."

"Perhaps." She slipped from Jane's grasp. "Once this passes through the gossip chain, what will people think?"

"I do not know." Jane rose and laid a hand on her shoulder. "Your means might be criticized, but none may condemn your motive. I choose to believe we reap what we sow. Good will come from this."

"I hope you are right." She screwed her eyes shut.

Jane licked her lips. "What is your opinion of Lydia—"

"Staying with Mrs. Forster?" Elizabeth led them to the chairs by the fireplace. "To say I am horrified—" She hugged a pillow to her chest. "Lydia is out of control. I cannot fathom how Colonel Forster will keep her in check." Elizabeth propped her chin on the overstuffed pillow. "Papa had no inclination to discuss the matter at dinner and now…" Her voice seized. Fickle, fickle tears, now that she needed to speak, they made themselves available. She gulped a breath and forced them into submission. "He is so cross he will not receive me now."

"He expects more from Colonel Forster than we do. Perhaps his understanding exceeds ours. We should trust him." Jane picked at the pillow's fringe.

Elizabeth dropped her head into the pillow. "I am not honoring him, am I?"

"Not everything must rest on our shoulders alone. I choose to trust this will work out for good as Aunt Gardiner said."

"I admire your faith."

"Come." Jane pulled her to her feet. "When your disposition becomes this morose, the only thing for it is sleep." She tucked Elizabeth under the counterpane. "Goodnight."

Elizabeth remained restless. Serenity was Jane's virtue, not hers. She would find a way to respect Papa and still help him recognize the great danger Lydia's behavior posed.

CHAPTER 6

Clanging bells called them to church. The squat stone building opened welcoming arms at the intersection of three lanes, on the outskirts of Longbourn. A small crowd milled around the door but parted to allow the Bennet ladies inside. People stood clustered in the aisles, exchanging Sunday pleasantries. A light breeze filtered through sunny windows. Elizabeth strained to catch snippets of conversation. No mention of Nash or Sterling, not yet, at least.

Charlotte pushed through the narrow aisle, Maria close on her heels. "I am so glad to see you." She clasped Elizabeth's hands and drew her close enough to whisper, "We heard what happened in town yesterday. Mama wanted you to know she is pleased. She has found Mr. Sterling endlessly troublesome."

Elizabeth's knees threatened to melt. She grabbed the nearest pew.

Charlotte turned to Mary. "Mama visited the Blacks yesterday. Mrs. Black is still weak, of course, and I doubt she will be at church today, but she is considerably better than the day we called. Her mother said they no longer fear for her life."

"Welcome news, indeed." Mary beamed. She slipped her arm in Elizabeth's and steadied her. "I had wondered how she fared."

"Your visit pleased them very much. Mrs. Black and her mother found you most charming, and in possession of the qualities most desirable in the sick room." Charlotte shriveled into an old woman's hunch. "They was jest lovey ladies, ya know. Not too cheery ta' bring a heart to fear for its life, not so somber that ya think yaself already dead. Jest like a ray o' sun." She grinned so much like the toothless woman that Elizabeth did a double take.

"I took a new book of herbal recipes from the library," Mary said. "I found recipes Lady Lucas has never mentioned—"

"Bring the book next time you visit. Few enterprises please her better than learning new plant lore. Neither Maria nor I have a head for herbs." Charlotte beckoned Lady Lucas with a nod.

Maria giggled. "She gets so cross with me. I cannot tell one leaf from another. They are all green, are they not?"

Mary quivered and coughed, but Elizabeth heard her snicker beneath it.

Elizabeth squeezed Mary's arm and winked.

Mr. Pierce approached the pulpit. They filed into their pews, the Lucases behind the Bennets.

"Good morning, girls." Lady Lucas pressed close to her daughters as the male Lucases slipped in beside her. "Mrs. Bennet is absent this morning?"

"She feels poorly and could not leave her chambers." Jane peeked at Elizabeth.

"I am sorry. Should I call this afternoon?"

"Thank you, Lady Lucas," Elizabeth said. "My father prepares to leave on a journey tomorrow. I doubt Mama will be well enough for callers amidst the excitement."

"Of course, I quite understand, dear." Lady Lucas smiled and eased onto the pew. "Perhaps tomorrow or the next day."

Mr. Bennet arrived at the family pew. The girls scooted to accommodate him.

Mr. Pierce read the banns.

Maria leaned forward to whisper in Kitty's ear, "He has the most soothing voice."

"He does. If only he were as pleasant to look at as to listen to."

"He is strange though. Why does he write his own sermons instead of preaching from the sermon books?"

"Hush." Mary hissed.

Kitty rolled her eyes and sat a little straighter.

" 'Who can find a virtuous woman? For her price is far above rubies.' We find these words in the tenth verse of the thirty-first chapter of Proverbs." Mr. Pierce lifted his head from his book.

Elizabeth studied his profile. His eyebrows were too heavy and his nose too prominent to be considered handsome, even by those who liked him best. She shot a quick glance at Mary. The warm cadence of his voice somehow erased those impressions and left every young woman and many of the older ones yearning to hear more.

"Further on, we read her husband has full confidence in her and lacks nothing of value. She brings him good, not harm, all the days of her life."

Low murmurs of assent flowed across the room.

"How confused our priorities." Mr. Pierce's brow furrowed. "It seems the way of men now is to search for a woman worth more than rubies. Later, he hopes she is of noble character."

Papa slid his hand over Elizabeth's and laced his fingers in hers. She met his gaze for the first time since dinner the previous evening. He blinked and lifted his lips into the barest of smiles. A horrible pressure left her chest. She pressed her head on his shoulder.

· • ·☙❧· • · ·☙❧· • · ·☙❧· • · ·☙❧· • · ·☙❧· • ·

After service ended, Mary and Papa enjoyed the society of their neighbors on the church grounds while Mr. Pierce closed the church. Papa whispered in Mary's ear. She nodded, cheeks tingling. They walked toward the church door and waited until the last of the parishioners left Mr. Pierce's company.

"Would you care to join us for tea this afternoon?" Papa asked.

"Thank you, sir." Mr. Pierce tipped his hat with a sidelong peek at Mary. "Your family's hospitality is always most appreciated. Your Mrs. Hill makes the best pies."

"Very good then." Mr. Bennet peered into the dissipating crowd. "Excuse me a moment, I need a word with Phillips." He turned to Mary. "Collect your sisters and go on with Mr. Pierce. I shall join you soon."

Lydia bounced up to him. "Maria invited me to take tea at Lucas Lodge this afternoon. I do so wish to go, please." She clasped her hands and blinked at him.

Mary swallowed a sigh. Those big pleading eyes virtually guaranteed Lydia would get her way. Only by the greatest self-control did she avoid the eye roll Papa detested. If he would just avoid indulging Lydia.

Papa wrinkled his lips and exhaled heavily. "I suppose so."

"Thank you, Papa." Lydia popped to her tiptoes and kissed his cheek. She flashed a victorious grin at her sisters and scurried after the Lucases.

Tea would be more enjoyable without Lydia vying for Mr. Pierce's attention. Though Lydia had no interest in being a clergyman's wife, she detested Mr. Pierce's attentions going to the plainest Bennet sister, not the liveliest.

"Excuse me." Mr. Bennet hurried off.

Pierce turned to Mary and bowed. "Might I escort you home, Miss Mary?"

"Yes, thank you." The intensity of his gaze heated her cheeks. She would have distrusted the attentions of a handsomer man, but Mr. Pierce's plainness worked to his advantage. She could not so easily dismiss him.

He nestled her hand in the crook of his elbow and guided them toward Mary's favorite path, lined with ancient tress to canopy the well-trodden dirt with an air of private solemnity. "I hear Mr. Bennet is planning a trip?"

"Yes, to Kent, with my uncle." Mary dared a brief glance at him. His delighted mien caught her off guard, tripping her heart into a full out tumble. No one ever had beheld plain Mary Bennet with so much regard. She should look away. Unable to break free, she smiled. If only it might be a lovely demure expression, like Jane's. Not a brash, vulgar one like Lydia's. Pierce winked, and she stumbled over a mote of dust.

He steadied her, eyes crinkling. A single dimple decorated his left cheek, heretofore unseen. "I wish him a most pleasant trip." He covered her hand with his. "May I speak to you of a subject of a most delicate nature? I would like to speak to your father—actually, I have several matters to discuss with him." His voice turned somber. "One in particular I wish your opinion on."

Mary's thoughts crashed into one another, rolled about and came to a screeching halt. For a moment she could barely put one foot in front of the other. The recent giddy warmth drained away, replaced by an odd, prickly feeling. "Certainly, I am most content to listen." The words left a dry, wooly residue on her tongue.

"Please remember, faithful are the wounds of a friend. I am a friend to you and your family."

"What are you trying to tell me?" Her voice squeaked. How ridiculous she sounded. No wonder so few listened to her. She tried to swallow the fuzziness on her tongue. It lodged in her throat.

"In town yesterday, at the coffeehouse, a group of officers sat at the table nearest me. I overheard their conversation." His brows pulled low over his eyes, and his voice dropped to a whisper.

Mary bit her lip. What would he need to discuss in such hushed tones?

He patted her hand, forehead creased with the deep lines of a very serious topic. "They discussed their impressions of several young women they had met in town."

Her breath hitched.

"Worse still, they went on to name your youngest sister among their acquaintances. I am concerned those young ladies may be in danger from their dishonorable intentions." He grimaced and looked skyward. "They took bets on which one of them would be first to tap one of the girls,[13] for they thought them all short heeled wenches[14]." Pierce's ears flushed brightly.

---

[13] Tap a girl: be the first to seduce her
[14] Short-heeled girl: a girl likely to fall on her back

Mary gasped and bit her knuckle. Confound it all, Lydia would ruin everything.

"I did not want to be the one to tell you…" Their eyes met, and his voice trailed off.

"We cannot protect her if we do not know what is happening." Mary picked at the strings of her bonnet. He would now tell her—so kindly, so gently—a man in his position could not be too careful about the company he kept. He must quit her acquaintance. She would be brave and maintain her dignity. Of course, he had little choice—

"What is your opinion? Should I speak to your father? What should I say to him?"

She blinked, brows drawn together in a tight little knot.

Pierce started and shook his head. "You do not think I meant to say…"

Mary shrugged. "I…I…do not…"

"Oh, by no means. I would never." A hint of his former smile returned. "You do not know him, but heaven forbid you should judge me by the actions of my elder brother."

Her eyes burned, and she blinked rapidly lest a tear escape. She managed to lift the corner of her lips.

"So…your father?"

Mary looked over her shoulder. "Lizzy, please, come here."

Lizzy hurried to Mary's side, cheeks bright. *Oh, dear.* She had overheard. Mary asked Mr. Pierce to repeat his tale anyway. No need to draw attention to Lizzy's foibles.

Pierce pressed Mary's hand. "In light of the severity of the situation, I believe I have a duty to talk to your father."

Lizzy chewed her lower lip and walked again. Her brow furrowed, and she blinked several times in rapid succession. "You are right. Papa needs to know."

Mary touched her elbow. "You are the best one to tell him." Her eyes bounced from Lizzy to Pierce. "Papa is exceedingly protective of his family, and I fear he will not hear those concerns easily."

Lizzy drew in an especially deep breath and offered Pierce a vulnerable half smile. "I might be able to get him to listen."

"Though Papa is generally phlegmatic, some few topics are apt to set him off." Mary's shoulders sagged a little. "He is prone to heed Lizzy more than anyone else."

Mama was not alone in having a favorite child. Unlike Lydia, Lizzy did not lord her status over her sisters. She reigned with humility and so lessened the sting to those not so favored.

Pierce ground the heel of his boot into the dirt. "I would gladly do the job myself—"

Lizzy shook her head. "No. Mary is right. I have the best chance to get Papa to listen."

"If I may be of service to your family in any way, say the word."

"Thank you, Mr. Pierce. You will excuse me, I…"

"Of course." He bowed.

Elizabeth hurried ahead. They followed at a moderate pace, dirt and leaves swirled in time to their steps.

"Thank you for your concern for us."

He cleared his throat. "I am glad your father invited me this afternoon. I am most anxious for a particular conversation with him. If you are agreeable."

She blushed all the way to the neckline of her gown. "I am."

·•·❧❧·•·❧❧·•·❧❧·•·❧❧·•·❧❧·•·

Several hours later, Mr. Pierce called Elizabeth to the bookroom and took his leave. The door swung open under the pressure of her soft knocks. Papa stood near the front window, hands clasped behind his back.

"Come in, Lizzy." He did not turn to look at her.

That was never a good sign. She swallowed hard.

"Close the door behind you and make sure it latches. I do not wish to be disturbed."

What did Mr. Pierce say? She swallowed sour anxiety. Surely Papa could not be angry with her for what the curate heard in town? Or did he believe she had sent Mr. Pierce to talk to him? She pressed the door shut and tested the latch.

"Sit child, and do be sure to breathe now and again. Fresh air will do your frame of mind no end of good."

A sharp gasp, half giggle and half relief, rushed out as she dropped onto her favorite footstool. Still stationed at the window, he clucked his tongue and nodded. Chin on her fists, elbows on knees, she waited.

Papa favored carefully prepared words. Few allowed him the luxury and were much poorer for it. Patience was a small price to pay for his conversation.

He grumbled under his breath and took to his favorite chair, tapping his fingertips together in front of his chest.

Cold prickles spread along the back of her neck. "What did Mr. Pierce say?"

His lips flashed upward in a parody of a smile and resumed their previous frown. "He did not want to linger because you needed to speak with me." He glared at her with eyes that threatened to turn her into a little girl.

"Oh, Papa." She fisted her skirt into wrinkles. Hill would scold her later.

"You do not approve of Lydia's stay with Mrs. Forster."

"No, sir," she whispered.

"You are troubled by Carver's talk and by what Pierce heard in town." He drummed his fingers together.

"He told you?"

"His conscience would not allow him to leave the disagreeable task to you."

She did not need to check. He wore that expression, the one from last night. The one that meant she disappointed him. The one she never wanted to see again. The scuffed toes of her slippers peeked from under her skirts. Perhaps Mattie—

"Look at me, child."

Must he use the voice she could not resist? Angst poised, ready to strike her vein. She chewed her bottom lip and peeked up.

The right side of his mouth twitched, and his eyes, no longer thunderhead grey, twinkled, light as the morning mist.

Tension drained away so fast, the room spun just a little. She mustered a weak smile.

"Do not make yourself uneasy, my love." He stroked the back of her hand with his thumb. "Wherever you and Jane are known, you must be respected and valued. You will not appear to less advantage for having a very silly sister. We shall have no peace at Longbourn if Lydia does not stay with Mrs. Forster. The colonel is a sensible man. He will keep her out of real mischief. She is luckily too poor to be an object of prey to anybody." He tipped up her chin. "Do not be troubled by the bluster of those prate roasts[15] at the coffee house. You do not understand the ways of young men. Trust me."

"What advantage can Lydia derive from the friendship of Mrs. Forster? The probability her imprudence will increase with such a companion is quite high." She hated it when words tumbled out before she censored them.

---

[15] prate roasts: talkative boys

"She is your mother's daughter, as you are mine. Your mother did well enough for herself. I trust your sister shall as well." He laughed and cocked a shaggy eyebrow. "I hope her visit with Mrs. Forster will help her appreciate the great latitude I allow her. At any rate, she cannot grow many degrees worse without authorizing us to lock her up for the rest of her life."

"What of the great disadvantage to us all which arises from the public notice of Lydia's unguarded and imprudent manner?"

"The Carver fellow?" he snorted. "Squeamish youths who cannot bear to be connected with a little absurdity are not worth regret. He is as windy a fellow as I have ever known, and no one of consequence pays the likes of him mind."

"What about Mr. Pierce?" She picked at the wrinkles in her skirt, her eyes on the crushed fabric, not him.

"He is a most attentive neighbor, and I appreciate his well-intended concern. However, it is my role to know what is best for my family. Though a bit coarse, I admit, Colonel Forster is a sensible man and good guardian to his wife. He will be to Lydia as well." His fingertips pressed firmly into her hand, enough to be barely uncomfortable. Papa leaned forward. "Look at me."

She lifted her head and drew in a sharp breath. The storm clouds returned to his eyes.

"Do not question me any further in this."

"Yes, Papa." She did not wait to be dismissed and fled from the room before the burning in her eyes overflowed.

A sprint up the stairs helped clear her mind. Papa was not insensible to the situation. They merely disagreed as to its nature. He considered Colonel Forster more capable and Lydia less troublesome than she did. Even if no disaster came of Lydia's stay with Mrs. Forster, she would still come home as the same foolish girl she left.

That Elizabeth could work on, but it would require some thought. She found her half-boots and slipped them on. Walking helped her think.

·•·ᏰᏇᏄ·•·ᏰᏇᏄ·•·ᏰᏇᏄ·•·ᏰᏇᏄ·•·ᏰᏇᏄ·•·

"Mattie!"

Elizabeth cringed. Lydia's voice pierced the early morning air without consideration for who still slept. Why would that matter? The world, after all, revolved around Lydia. Elizabeth snorted and cracked the dressing room door to peek out.

"Mattie!" Lydia stood in the middle of the hallway clad only in her nightgown. She turned in circles, flapping her arms. "Mattie, where are you? I need you now."

"Hush!" Elizabeth hissed. "You will disturb Mama."

"My bonnets are not packed." Lydia stamped her bare foot and stormed toward the staircase.

Elizabeth shut the door softly and leaned against the door jam, eyes closed. Pages rustled, and a pencil scratched on paper, while whispered voices conferred. She opened her eyes. Jane, Mary and Kitty shared the bed with open books and loose paper, attentive as schoolgirls under a strict headmistress.

"Do you think Hill uses bread to clean wallpaper?" Mary pointed to a smudged page in their new favorite tome.

"I have never seen the girls do so." Jane scribbled a quick note.

The door flew open. Lydia flew across the room and dropped on the bed, crushing papers and bouncing books.

"Jane, Lizzy! Why do you not help me prepare? Mattie does nothing right, and I must be ready when Colonel Forster comes. He is so stern about promptness. I cannot understand what it matters." Lydia panted.

"You were packed last night. What happened?" Elizabeth braced for the storm.

"I did not like the way Mattie folded my gowns. I unpacked them all, so she can do better." Lydia tossed her head. Her unbound curls bobbed. "Kitty, you should help me. All of you should."

"She is not your servant, Lyddie." Jane stood and mustered something akin to a glare. "Nor are we."

Lydia's eye bulged, and her face transformed from merely flushed to raincloud violet.

"She shares my room. My concerns are hers."

Kitty snorted and followed with several more unladylike noises.

"She ought to help me for she is older than me. After all, she has nothing better to do with her time. It is not as if she, or any of you for that matter, is going anywhere." Lydia stamped in a circle to glower at each of her sisters in turn.

They shrugged at one another and returned to their books.

"Why does no one help me?" Lydia slammed the library book shut.

"This is your trip and your responsibility. You disrupted your trunks. Go pack—we have other things to do." Mary opened the book again.

"You are jealous and do not want me to go." Lydia's fists shook at her sides. "You are horrible—every one of you." She tugged at Kitty's sleeve. "You must come."

Kitty pulled against her too hard, and Lydia let go. Kitty tumbled into Mary.

"Indeed, we will not." Elizabeth helped Kitty right herself. "If you continue to waste time arguing with us, you will have no time to pack. We must go to breakfast now." She scooted past Lydia and beckoned her sisters.

Elizabeth waited in the doorway for the rest of her sisters to pass. Lydia stood alone in the middle of the room muttering language a young lady had no business knowing, let alone using. She shut the door.

Lyddie would get used to this as would her sisters. No more bowing to her demands. No more living under her rule. No more resentment. No doubt, Lydia would fight every step of the way. Their resolve would remain.

Elizabeth caught up with her sisters on the landing, and they entered the dining room together. Papa grunted a greeting, head buried in his newspaper.

Staccato stomps pounded the stairs.

Papa folded his paper noisily and slipped it beside his plate.

Lydia marched into the dining room, dressed, her hair still unbound. "Lord, I am so hungry." She dropped into her seat, breathed deeply and reached for the nearest platter.

"Good morning to you," Papa spoke through clenched teeth.

"Good morning, Papa." Lydia shoveled stewed fruit to her plate.

"Are you finished packing?" Jane passed the porridge in her direction.

"No, I got that lollypoop, Mattie, back to finish the job." Lydia made a show of tucking her napkin into her lap. She looked from one sister to another, each turned away. "I do not understand why you cannot be happy for me. At least you might be Kitty, for you shall be alone in the room whilst I am gone."

"I cannot see why Mrs. Forster should not ask me as well as Lydia." Kitty crossed her arms and slouched. "Though I am not her particular friend, I have just as much right to be asked as she for I am two years older."

Lydia rolled her eyes. "You are not her particular friend." She patted her chest in something almost entirely unlike humility. "I am. After all, the most lively, agreeable companion of all of us."

"Lydia." Elizabeth balled her fists under the table. How foolish of her to believe Lydia's tantrum concluded simply because they left the room.

Jane set her glass down more firmly than necessary. "Lyddie, do not be unkind."

What? A firm note in Jane's voice? Pride filled her, and she would have hugged Jane right there and then if she could.

Papa's eyebrows arched. He turned to Elizabeth, chin balanced on his knuckles.

"I am not unkind. Mrs. Forster likes me above everyone else. She will go away to Brighton soon and leave me behind. We must make the most of our remaining time together." She blinked innocently at Jane. "Kitty hardly knows what to say to the officers. How merry is a tongued tied—"

"It is only because *you* never stop talking. If you would take a moment to breathe, perhaps someone else might have a share of the conversation." Kitty stared into her plate, chin quivering.

"I am an obliging guest, entertaining with my stories—"

"Lyddie, you would be wise to listen—" Mary clutched the edge of the table

"Wise. What do I care about wise? Wise is dull and drab." Lydia bounced out of her seat and danced behind her sisters. "I wish to be merry and bright and winsome and gay."

Papa pulled the napkin from his collar and slammed it on the table. "Enough, Lydia. You would do well to sit down. This is not a ballroom."

"How droll you are, Papa." She laughed as she returned to her chair. "Surely you do not object to my excitement for you told me I might go."

"I fear you will never be easy till you expose yourself in some public place or other." He cleared his throat.

Elizabeth jumped and shot him a sidelong look. At least his ire focused on Lydia, not her.

Lydia blinked and shook her head. A slow smile bloomed. "What a good joke, Papa. I simply wish to enjoy myself as Mama tells me to do." She sneered down her nose at Kitty. "While you make do here, with only our sisters to entertain you."

"Oh!" Kitty bolted from the table and slammed the door.

Mary sagged against the back of her chair and threw her napkin on the table.

"She should not be so sensitive." Lydia shrugged and vigorously stirred her porridge. "I only spoke what everyone thinks already. What is so bad in that?" Lydia slurped her teacup loudly.

"Oh, Lyddie." Jane cringed and pressed the bridge of her nose. "You may not rightly understand what everyone truly thinks."

"Hardly." Lydia sneered over her muffin.

"I suggest you restrain yourself lest I reconsider this trip of yours." He pushed away from the table and towered over Lydia. "You will join me in my bookroom as soon as you are finished eating."

• • ᏬᎠᏬ • • ᏬᎠᏬ • • ᏬᎠᏬ • • ᏬᎠᏬ • • ᏬᎠᏬ • •

The chimes rang, and Lydia dashed from the study, chattering about Forster arriving soon. Bennet removed his glasses and pinched the bridge of his nose. Just as well. Her babble had obscured his most fervent admonitions.

How could his youngest take after her aunt and her grandmother before her? No other women talked so long, nor so fast as Edith Phillips and Amelia Gardiner. Why did she not take after her Uncle Gardiner instead?

If only he might stay home and manage Lydia himself. Naturally Collins's noble patroness would not be gainsaid. His business would be conducted on her timetable, what matter that she be wholly unconnected with them?

"Gah!" He pushed himself up from his chair, knees popping.

Turning Lydia over to a relative stranger vexed him more that the disagreeable business with Collins and his honorable Lady patroness. Surely though, a colonel of the militia could control the girl's silliness better than her sisters. He rubbed his temples, ears ringing the way they always did in the wake of a conversation with most of the Gardiner women.

The front door creaked open and shut again. Lydia squealed. That would be the Forster's arrival. He plodded to the porch where Lydia already waited.

"Here they come, Papa." She clutched his arm. "Where are my sisters? Where is Mama? How dreadful, no one is here to see me off. Are they not happy for me?"

"No, I do not think so."

She huffed. "They are jealous old tabbies."

"Hardly." He grumbled low in his throat and thumbed his lapels. "I believe your sisters are tired of your gloating and high-handed ways."

"Kitty is far too sensitive. You said it yourself."

He cringed. Confound it all, he should never have uttered that in her hearing.

"She should be happy for me. If she had true sisterly feelings…" Lydia crossed her arms so tightly her shoulders rounded.

"When have you ever exerted yourself to be helpful to her?"

"I am the youngest. They are supposed to take care of me. Oh, it is so unfair. Why does Mama not make—"

"Your mother is unwell." He clasped his hands behind his back. "Did you take your leave of her this morning?"

"Look! They are here." She dashed out meet the Forster's carriage.

He closed his eyes and sighed. Her selfishness would not be cured this morning, but cured it would be. The colonel's voice drew him from his reverie. He tugged his coat sleeves and trudged down the steps to join them.

A quarter of an hour later, the carriage pulled away. Three pairs of eyes peeked through the window. He chuckled under his breath. They might have the appearance of grown up ladies, but they remained his little girls. A man should want sons. A son would have spared him the unpleasant business with Collins. Still, he would not trade away any one of his girls for an heir.

They waited for him in the foyer.

"Will you be away soon, Papa?" Jane asked. "Can we prepare a basket for you and Uncle?"

"I dread the food at public houses." He smiled though the effort took all his strength. "A basket would be delightful."

Jane and Mary hurried toward the kitchen.

"You look so tired, Papa," Lizzy said softly. She put her small hand on his arm and squeezed.

"I hate to be away from home." He covered her fingers with his and savored the warmth. "Take care of your mama whilst I am gone. Do not allow your Aunt Phillips to be left alone with her."

"Yes, sir."

"If you have issues with the tenants, call for Pierce. He will be able to assist you."

"Yes, sir."

"If you need anything, send an express. You know where I left the directions—"

"Yes, sir." She laid her head against his shoulder.

He patted her cheek. "Forster is no fool. He understands."

She pressed his arm. "You are doing your best to take care of us all."

How did she always say the right things?

"I am sure it will all work out."

He sighed and kissed the top of her head. He would do everything in his power to ensure she was right.

CHAPTER 7

Elizabeth prepared for her errands in town. Jane finalized plans for next month's dinner party with Hill. Mary and Kitty, baby dresses in hand, had left an hour earlier. Eight days into Papa's trip, and their adventures in household management, Longbourn remained standing. No kitchen crises, no raised voices, no demonstrations in the streets of Meryton. With all the earlier excitement, Longbourn's current quietude pleased her.

The fresh morning air helped her ignore the nagging tension, a persistent companion that teased the loose hairs at the back of her neck. On the outskirts of Meryton, she encountered Mrs. Black, perched, crab-like, on a large roadside rock.

"Are you well?" Elizabeth crouched beside the old woman.

"Thank you kindly for asking, Missy Bennet. Just a'resting the old bones a bit. The trip into town gets longer each year." Mrs. Black's cold fingers patted her hand. "Can you help an old body up?"

Elizabeth handed her a rough carved cane and helped her pull to her feet. Mrs. Black teetered until she planted the cane firmly. She craned her neck, lips pulled into a toothless smile. "Thank you kindly."

"My pleasure." Elizabeth offered the bent woman her arm. How did Mrs. Black walk this far on her own?

"You be good folk, Missy Bennet." Mrs. Black shuffled. A cloud of dirt surrounded her feet. "What with all the to-do in town and the officers, I just think you ought to hear."

Elizabeth froze mid-step. Her cheeks chilled, as cold as Mrs. Black's hands.

"You Bennets ain't all romping[16] girls. No, most of you are right proper ladies, I say."

The world wavered around her. Elizabeth clung to Mrs. Black, and they both tottered. How did one react to such a declaration? Should she be pleased her reputation might avoid tarnish from Lydia, or horrified by her implications about Lydia?

"You ain't like those society misses who care for naught but themselves. Gentlefolk can afford to be cheated if you don't mind me saying. You told Sterling what to do with his thievin' ways, and you know what come of it? Sterling didn't want no more trouble. He

---

[16] Romping girls: forward, wanton girls

give me my last order freeman's quay[17]. With my daughter-in-law devilish sick and the apothecary bill, you know, we don't have the balsam[18] to spare. You done us a real good turn, Missy Bennet." She patted Elizabeth's hand. "Thank you kindly for your arm. I'll be on my way." Mrs. Black trundled toward the nearest shop.

Her reassurances were not a reason to rejoice. Hers were one woman's opinions, and she was not a woman of high standing. The gentlefolk of Meryton might still view Elizabeth's actions as dimly as they did Lydia's. The Bennet sisters could not relax their efforts—no, if anything, they must be redoubled.

•ᐧᔐᢀ•ᐧᔐᢀᐧ•ᐧᔐᢀ•ᐧᔐᢀᐧ•ᐧᔐᢀᐧ••

Just before teatime, Elizabeth wandered into the sitting room and dropped into a chair. Afternoon sun poured through the windows, a bit too warm and a bit too bright for comfort. She threw her head back and her arm over her face. Every encounter in town left her to speculate if they shared Mrs. Black's opinion: 'You ain't *all* romping girls'. The now permanent knot in her stomach loosened enough to allow a wave of bile into her throat. Not *all* the Bennets. What cold comfort. The weight on her chest pushed out a heavy sigh.

---

[17] Freeman's quay: free of expense
[18] Balsam: money

Soft steps entered the room with the swish of a skirt. A body lowered into the nearby chair. *Jane*. Only she moved so quietly.

"Are you well, Lizzy?"

"Well enough. You will be pleased. Someone in town agrees with you," Elizabeth muttered from beneath her arm and told Jane of her conversation with Mrs. Black.

Jane perched on the arm of Elizabeth's chair. "So we are right proper ladies? No one has called us that before."

Elizabeth snorted. "Mama would not consider it the compliment Mrs. Black did."

"I imagine not." Jane reached into her pocket. "This just came from the Forsters." She extended a neatly penned note, drenched in lilac scent. "A dinner party invitation for Thursday evening."

"This week? As in two days from now?" Elizabeth pushed herself upright with her elbows. "Do you think…"

"This bears all the hallmarks of Lydia's guidance." Jane shut her eyes and shook her head.

How better to conceal mischief? A dinner party would provide Lydia every opportunity to expose herself. Colonel Forster would never suspect the danger a social event could afford.

Elizabeth huffed. "I dread the effects of our youngest sister's influence."

"Mama works for weeks planning even a small gathering." Jane set the letter aside. "Mrs. Forster is so young, and her family was in trade. I doubt she has any idea of how to conduct a proper dinner."

"This will be a disaster." Elizabeth grimaced.

"I could offer to help."

"You know as well as I, Lydia will not accept. Do not place you self in the way of such abuse." Elizabeth scoured her face with her palms. "We should be glad for the opportunity to curb Lydia's behavior during the party."

"Poor Mrs. Forster." Jane brushed her bottom lip with her fist.

"At least she will be fortunate enough to take leave of us when the regiment departs for Brighton." Elizabeth rubbed her upper arms. "Whatever disgrace comes will not follow her long. What joy is hers."

Kitty burst in, breathless. "Maria told me about the Forster's dinner. Surely you will not decline the invitation—"

"Pause for breath occasionally." Elizabeth flung her arm across her eyes. Would that she might hide so easily from the coming disaster.

"Yes, we shall go." Jane nodded. Her smile spoke nothing of their earlier conversation.

How could it be—Jane's serenity never faltered. Not in the flutterings of Mama's nerves. Not in the midst of Lydia's tantrums. Not in the presence of the ill-mannered Carver. Even if she were not the most beautiful sister, people would deem her so for her ever-present tranquility.

"What fun!"

Elizabeth lifted her arm enough to peer under. Kitty bounced like a little girl on her first holiday.

"What will you wear?" Kitty ducked and caught Elizabeth's eye.

Elizabeth lowered her arm and raked loose hair from her face. "Would you like a project?"

Kitty's eyes sparkled. "May I work on your sprigged muslin?"

"You can hardly make it worse." Elizabeth chuckled and caught Kitty's hands. "You only have two days—"

"Plenty of time, you will see." Kitty scurried upstairs.

"I am glad someone is pleased." Jane looked at the empty doorway.

"Poor dear, she must bear the happiness for us all."

· • ᖇᖇ · • • ᖇᖇ · • · ᖇᖇ · • · ᖇᖇ · • • ᖇᖇ • ·

Two nights later, Elizabeth twisted and turned in front of her dressing room mirror. "Kitty, how did you transform my ghastly frock into *this*? Are you sure you do not want to wear your creation yourself? For all the work—"

"I tailored the fit to you." Kitty tweaked a seam straight. "Besides, I adore my blue one."

"You may provoke Jane to envy with this. I expect you will style her gowns soon."

Kitty clapped and squealed. "I already made plans for her green one."

"Go call Mattie to help you with your hair. We need to leave soon."

"We will not be late tonight." Kitty smoothed Elizabeth's skirt one last time. "Lydia is the one we always wait on."

A half hour later, the Bennet carriage departed for Meryton. Kitty's constant stream of upbeat conversation provided a pleasant distraction from Elizabeth's anxiety. Surely Kitty never said so much in an entire week as she did during this one carriage ride— another effect of Lydia's absence? Best Kitty indulge now, once at the Forster's, she would be unlikely to get another word in crossways.

The driver handed them out and took the coach to a convenient spot to wait for their departure. A uniformed lieutenant bowed them inside. Lydia and Mrs. Forster waited in the foyer.

The closet-like space closed in around Elizabeth. Foreboding lurked in the abundant shadows. She pulled in a deep breath. Bad architecture should not be blamed on their hostess.

"I told you they would be the first to arrive." Lydia clutched Mrs. Forster's arm. She leaned forward and exposed her ample décolletage. "A little late is more fashionable than a little early."

Elizabeth ignored Lydia's batting eyes. Could Lydia even see clearly when she did that? "Thank you for your invitation, Mrs. Forster."

"I am so happy you came. I cannot tell you how I depended on Lydia to make this a memorable evening." Mrs. Forster beamed at Lydia.

Elizabeth pressed her stomach and struggled not to roll her eyes.

"Your dress—" Kitty touched the deep emerald, lace-trimmed sleeve.

"Harriet insisted I borrow something of hers for tonight." Lydia twirled. "I told you they would be jealous."

"You need a lace tucker." Mary crossed her arms and scowled.

"The gown is lovely —" Jane wet her lips and pressed them hard.

"You are hardly the same shape as Mrs. Forster." Kitty plucked Lydia's bodice seam. She peeked at Mrs. Forster. "Are you not concerned she will tear these seams? One deep breath and I fear—"

"What do you know?" Lydia snatched the dress from Kitty's hand and sidled close to Elizabeth. "Your new gown is lovely, Lizzy. I thought Papa said not to place new orders in his absence." She wagged her finger.

Jealousy made an unattractive accessory for Mrs. Forster's frock. "This is my old sprigged muslin. Kitty remade it. Remember, she did your pink one, too. You should honor her and wear it tonight. The color suits you well. I will help you change."

Kitty's mouth hung agape. She shook her head violently and edged behind Mary.

"Lizzy is quite right." Mary slipped forward and pressed her shoulder to Elizabeth's.

"No." Lydia leaned toward them, her gown ready to overflow.

"Kitty worked quite hard on your dress." Jane reached for Lydia's arm, but she jerked away.

"This outfit is new, sewn by a proper modiste, not by my sister." Lydia wrapped her arms under her bosom. Her face flushed. "I want to wear this." She quivered and sucked a large gulp of air.

Elizabeth and Mary cringed. The first scream of Lydia's tantrums was always the worst.

Jane stepped forward and laid an arm over Lydia's shoulders. "What are your plans for dinner?"

The red blotches faded from Lydia's cheeks. She smoothed her bodice and composed her features into a poor rendition of a smile. "Come and see what a smart dinner awaits us." She turned and beckoned them all to follow.

Elizabeth lingered back and shared a pained glance with Mary. Lydia was in rare form tonight. A mere colonel would not be able to rein her in. The task required a brigadier general, at the very least.

They entered a large room nearly devoid of furniture. A few chairs waited, scattered along the walls, and a pianoforte stood, lonely, in the far corner. Their footsteps echoed off the bare floor. Faded boards pointed to an absent carpet.

"You will sit here, Mary." Lydia patted the pianoforte bench. "We thoughtfully placed the pianoforte near the window for your comfort. So many dancing couples will make the room stuffy."

"Excuse me?" Mary retreated and bumped into Elizabeth.

"I said you shall sit here." Red patches speckled Lydia's forehead.

"Why ever for?"

"To play the pianoforte, silly. What else?" Lydia laughed, an annoying, bark, reminiscent of Lady Lucas's pug.

"You expect me to play—all evening? Like a concert?" Mary's voice stretched thin enough to tear on the breeze carried through narrowly open windows.

"How else are we to dance?"

"Lydia," Mary folded her arms. "It is customary to *ask* someone to play, not demand. To focus all the attention on myself is immodest and rude. I will not do so."

Lydia drew a ragged breath. Her ears flushed crimson.

Mrs. Forster wrapped her arm in Lydia's. "Miss Mary, you play so well. Would you privilege us with your music?" She batted her eyes.

Lydia certainly taught her that tactic.

"I would be happy to play a set, or at most two."

Lydia's fist shook at her side. "You are disagreeable and jealous, and trying to ruin everything."

"Your plans must change." Mary set her lips in a firm line.

Jane patted Lydia's shoulder. "Many young ladies of our acquaintance would be pleased to perform."

"They will play only what they like." Lydia's mouth pursed into a well-practiced pout.

Mary drummed her fingers along the pianoforte's edge. "And I can be ordered about like some guild musician?"

"We want to dance tonight." Lydia stomped.

Elizabeth sighed. With all the stamping she did, the sole of Lydia's foot must be calloused.

Jane edged between Lydia and Mary. "You were going to show us the dining room." Jane turned Lydia toward the doorway.

Dear sweet Jane, the only one among them with gifts sufficient to manage Mama's nerves and Lydia's outbursts. A nugget of guilt fell into Elizabeth's heart. Why did she appreciate Jane's strength only now?

"I am sure you will approve, Miss Bennet." Mrs. Forster led the way.

Elizabeth gestured for Kitty to precede her and paused by Mary's side. "You can claim illness. I will call the carriage," she whispered.

Mary leaned her head on Elizabeth's shoulder. "I abhor falsehood. I cannot. Thank you for thinking of me though."

Did she do that enough? Mary so rarely complained, she was easy to forget. One more lump of guilt. Elizabeth rubbed Mary's back and helped her up. Arm in arm they traversed the makeshift ballroom.

"Where is the table?" Kitty gasped.

Elizabeth peeked over Kitty's shoulder. Sideboards and small tables bearing covered serving dishes, china, silverware and glasses lined the otherwise empty dining room.

"The servants moved it upstairs." Lydia tossed the thought away with a wave of her hand.

"Where shall we sit for dinner?" Kitty's mouth hung agape.

"I lack sufficient servants to attend so many guests at the table, so Lydia suggested a standing dinner." Mrs. Forster clapped her hands softly and beamed.

A servant approached and whispered to her mistress.

"Excuse me, a hostess must make sure everything is perfect for her guests." Mrs. Forster smiled and hurried after the maid.

Elizabeth grabbed Lydia's arm. "How could you suggest a standing supper? Mrs. Forster will be a laughingstock. No one serves a standing supper for a dinner party."

"Mrs. Goulding did two months ago." Lydia tapped her nose, brows lifted.

"Mrs. Goulding hosted a card party after the recital. Everyone had already eaten dinner. She served supper as courtesy to the late hour."

Lydia wrenched her arm away. "La! No one abides by that foolishness these days. Besides, they should be grateful for Mrs. Forster's invitation. Not a soul will notice. Standing suppers will become the newest rage. Mrs. Forster and I shall be fashion leaders." She spun and flounced away. Her footsteps echoed in the barren room.

The remaining Bennet sisters stared at each other.

"A standing supper?" Elizabeth croaked.

"And concert by Mary." Jane wrapped her arm in Mary's.

"With Lydia falling out of a dress too small to contain her rum dugs."[19]

Mary's eyes bulged. "Kitty! Such language."

Kitty lowered her eyes. The penitential moment ended when giggles bubbled out. Knuckles shoved in her mouth did not contain them. Soon they all wiped tears away for laughing so hard.

"A merry heart doeth good, like a medicine."[20] Mary dabbed the last drops from her cheek.

"I suppose the rest of the evening will demand one." Jane smoothed her skirts.

Elizabeth pressed her handkerchief to her cheeks. "Yes, it will." She tucked the handkerchief into her pocket and straightened her shoulders. "We shall do Mama and Papa proud, no matter Lydia's silliness."

They hugged each other quickly. Jane led them to join the newly arrived guests in the converted ballroom.

Mrs. Forster stood with Sir William and Lady Lucas, who snuck surreptitious glances at the barren room. Lydia and Maria chatted steps away. Charlotte beckoned Elizabeth, Jane and Mary.

---

[19] Rum dugs: fine breasts
[20] Prover bs 17:22

"I am afraid Mrs. Long sends her regrets. She and her daughters will be unable to attend tonight," Lady Lucas said.

"Oh dear. I fear a shortage of young ladies. The Smiths and the Bonds sent their regrets as well." Mrs. Forster sighed and slumped.

Mary's eyebrows rose high, and she turned to Elizabeth, who bit her lower lip and pressed her hand to her chest.

Lydia pulled Maria to Mrs. Forster. "I suppose we must be all the more entertaining." She looked at Maria, and they tittered.

The way Charlotte's mouth pinched, Lydia's suggestion must have tasted like vinegar. Lady Lucas called her away before she could comment further.

The main room slowly filled with a mix of officers and the denizens of Meryton. Mrs. Forster directed everyone to the dining room for dinner. An unpleasant murmur began at one end of the room, and quickly grew into a noisy hum as people about the furniture's whereabouts. Mrs. Forster instructed her guests to serve themselves for a standing supper. Silence echoed for three long heartbeats.

Mrs. Goulding leaned to Elizabeth, and whispered, "I shall die of embarrassment if anyone assumes I advised Mrs. Forster to host such a party."

Elizabeth's ears burned. She muttered something reassuring and slipped away.

The milling crowd impeded her progress. She bumped into someone, murmured an apology and sidled against the wall to be trapped between a screen and the dreaded Mrs. Jaw and Mrs. Jabber. At some point, Elizabeth had known their proper names, but they hardly signified. The sisters, as old as Meryton, knew everyone and their business. They strutted, old hens in a henhouse, squawking and scolding and difficult to tell apart, save for Mrs. Jaw's crooked nose and Mrs. Jabber's meaty jowls. Between them, they had more opinions than a hen had feathers.

Mrs. Jaw tugged at her sleeves and sniffed. "If she does not employ servants enough to serve a proper dinner, she should not have attempted a large gathering."

"I would be ashamed to present so few dishes for so many people." Mrs. Jabber waved her handkerchief with a flourish.

"Colcannon?[21] Served to guests? She should stick to hosting tea." Mrs. Jaw wrinkled her nose.

"I thought the Bennet girls helped her."

Elizabeth bit her tongue and edged further behind the painted screen. A drop of sweat trickled down the back of her neck.

"Mrs. Bennet is such an accomplished hostess." Mrs. Jabber tucked her handkerchief in her sleeve. "I can hardly fathom her daughters were involved in *this.*" She leaned close to her sister. "Mrs. Forster is full

---

[21] Colcannon: an Irish dish of potatoes and cabbage pounded together in a mortar then stewed with butter

young to be the wife of a senior officer. She does him no credit at all."

"Nor do his officers if you ask me." Mrs. Jaw stared down her nose at several nearby ensigns. "Look at them, shoving their way ahead of their betters. At least half of them are not gentlemen either."

Mrs. Jabber clutched her breast. "Do tell."

If only that little bit of news surprised Elizabeth as much as it seemed to surprise them.

"Take Lt. Denny, the one with Miss Lydia Bennet. Mrs. Long's cook told my housekeeper their butler talked to his man. Lt. Denny's family line contains not a single landowner, nor fortune of any sort. I heard his father did a good turn of some sort—"

"More likely his mother," Mrs. Jabber said from behind her hand.

"How wicked." Mrs. Jaw cackled. "But hardly unlikely. Anyway a favor of *some kind* was done for a local gentleman, and Mr. Denny found a place as a militia officer. He represents himself as heir to his father's estate when there is no estate at all. If I were Mrs. Bennet, I would keep my daughters far removed from the scoundrel, lest they throw themselves away on a man with nothing."

"Not that Lydia Bennet is a fine catch herself."

Elizabeth's breath hitched. Her fists clenched so tightly, her nails dug trenches into her palms.

Mrs. Jabber waved her handkerchief in Lydia's direction. "She possesses no dowry to speak of and, without her sisters' elegant manners and excellent character, she is little more than a game pullet."[22]

"I heard Mrs. Bond will not allow her daughters—"

Enough! If she listened to another word, Elizabeth would do something far worse than publicly call those two biddies Jaw and Jabber. She pressed through the milling assembly–anywhere to be away from them. Lydia stopped her in the center of the crowd. Lt. Denny prowled at Lydia's shoulder.

"Is this not wonderful, Lizzy?" She panned the room. "Everyone is enjoying themselves. I told you no one would be so droll as to object to a standing supper with such merry company available." She turned and beamed at Denny.

The stare he gave her in return spoke words most definitely not to be uttered in polite society. She tried to scrape the bitter bile off her tongue against the roof of her mouth. "Do not be so quick to judge, Lydia—"

"La! What do I care for their opinions? Denny and I think this a perfectly delightful party." She skipped away. Denny stalked behind, a wolf trailing his prey.

Elizabeth felt more than saw the dark looks following Lydia, and knew many fixed on her for the crime of being Lydia's sister. A hand on her shoulder made her jump.

"The servants say they will run out of food soon," Kitty whispered.

---

[22] Game pullet: a young whore or forward girl in the way of becoming one.

"What a fitting disaster on the heels of everything else." Elizabeth pinched the bridge of her nose.

"I suppose it is no loss. The food is tasteless. People say she must pay the cook pennies." Kitty sniggered.

Elizabeth braced herself against the wall. "No compliments on anything tonight?"

"Many complimented your gown...and mine." Kitty clasped her hands under her chin. "Lydia finds fault with everything I sew for her. I am sure she would not believe the rude remarks about her dress."

Elizabeth squeezed her eyes closed. When she opened them, Mary stood beside Kitty. Mr. Pierce hovered behind them, wings spread, alert for whatever might come. What a fine man, so protective on their behalf.

"Mary!" Lydia's shrill voice exploded from near the pianoforte. "Mary!"

"Perhaps we should go hear her." Elizabeth sighed.

"Not I." She will not give me a moment's peace if she notices me." Kitty darted through the crowd and disappeared.

"Mary!"

Heads turned and stares leveled at them. How did mere looks burn so?

Pierce escorted them through the room, lending them a small measure of respectability—or was that pity—as they crossed to the piano.

"The problem you caused is solved." Lydia smiled broadly and thrust her chest out a little farther.

Pierce faced the window.

"What problem?" Mary's cheeks glowed crimson.

"Our music problem, you goose." Lydia grinned, eyes slightly narrowed.

The hair on the back of Elizabeth's neck lifted.

"Miss Goulding agreed to play for us too, so you have not ruined everything. You shall play the first half of the evening, and she, the second."

"How kind of you to consult me." Mary's nostrils flared, her jaw tensed. "I told you, I will play two sets for you, and no more."

"Mr. Pierce." Lydia bounced to his side and wrapped her arm in his. She blinked at him. "You must convince Mary it is her Christian duty to play for us."

He pulled his neck back in a bird-like maneuver and peered down his beaky nose. "Excuse me?"

"The Good Book says 'Give to those who ask.'"[23]

His brows drew together as he pulled his arm from her grasp. "I will thank you not to contort the Good Book for your selfish ends. You well know those words mean something else."

Lydia huffed. "La! See what I care when people say you ruined their fun."

"Perhaps I should not play at all." Mary folded her arms.

Pierce flanked her with an expression that mirrored Mary's. Elizabeth bit her cheeks not to laugh.

---

[23] Luke 6:30

"You promised." Red blotches dotted Lydia's face and neck.

"Please, Miss Mary," Mrs. Forster said softly.

Mary glanced at Pierce who nodded with a frown. "I promised to play two sets, and I will." She sat at the bench.

"I will turn the pages for you." Mr. Pierce stationed himself between the pianoforte and the window.

Elizabeth smiled her thanks. *They would be a good match, if only*—

Lydia clapped and dragged Mrs. Forster to the center of the room where she announced something that was lost in the hum of the crowd.

"It is time for dancing," Lydia cried, chest heaving.

—if only Lydia did not cause some calamity in the meantime. Elizabeth groaned and covered her eyes. Mr. Pierce was a steady man, but everyone had their limits.

Lydia returned to Elizabeth. "Colonel Forster!" She waved him over. Shielding her face with her hand, she wrinkled her nose and sneered at her sister. "You will dance tonight. I will not have you stand around stupidly with all these officers about."

"At your service, Miss Lydia." Colonel Forster bowed.

"My sister needs an introduction. She has no partner to dance with."

Elizabeth's eyes bulged. "Sir…no…I…"

Colonel Forster glanced about and tapped the nearest uniformed man's shoulder. "May I present

Major Sloane as a most desirable partner, Miss Elizabeth." He gestured toward the major who bowed.

Lydia tossed a saucy grin and flounced away.

"Excuse me, Major." Elizabeth stepped a little closer to the colonel. "Forgive me, sir, this is all highly improper. Lydia takes too much on herself, and her exuberance needs to be curbed, lest her behavior reflect badly—"

"Your concern is touching, Miss Elizabeth." Colonel Forster laced his fingers atop his ample belly and looked down on her with an eye-crinkling smile. "It does you and your family credit."

She clenched her teeth. As a child, she had hated condescending elders who patted her head. The distaste had never faded.

"I maintain a whole regiment of soldiers. You can trust me to manage a fifteen-year-old girl." He laughed, belly jiggling. "I appreciate your concern, but do allow the poor girl some harmless fun. I will keep her out of trouble."

Head-patted children should not kick their elders in the shin, so Elizabeth replied, "Of course, sir. Forgive me for troubling you with so trifling a concern," in her quietest voice, curtsied and turned away.

Major Sloane appeared in front of her and bowed. "May I have the privilege of this dance?" His mustache twitched. He reminded her of a rabbit nibbling a purloined carrot.

Perhaps Major Rabbit would be safe enough for a single set. "Thank you, sir. I would be happy to dance."

He led her to the floor, hands cold and clammy. How she despised a partner with cold hands. At least her toes remained untrodden, and he kept rhythm well enough. They came to a pause in the dance, and, while waiting their turn, could not avoid some manner of conversation.

"Your sister is a right fine looking young lass." Sloane's eyes wandered toward Lydia. "I understand your father and uncle to be away for a prolonged trip."

She stiffened. "How are you aware of my family affairs, sir?"

"I mean no offense." He inclined his head. "I merely repeat what your sister told many of us." The gaze he bestowed on Lydia now fell to Elizabeth.

She inched away. How soon could she get home and bathe? Their turn came, and she focused on the dance steps. Thankfully, she changed partners several times, so she did not face Sloane again for a full five minutes.

"Have you a beau, Miss?" Sloane asked as he took her hand for a turn.

Elizabeth flushed, first hot, then sickly cold, unable to draw her hand from his fast enough. If only this set would end. Could Mary not play faster?

"We are not long in Meryton." He stepped back and bowed. "Your sister is a right entertaining lass, and it seems like you would be, too. Do you care—"

"Certainly not. You take far too many liberties, sir, and I would thank you to importune me no further."

Forgoing a final curtsey, she spun on her heel and hurried away.

Mr. Pierce intercepted her halfway to the pianoforte. "Are you well, Miss Elizabeth?"

"No, sir, I am not, not at all." She searched over her shoulder for any sign of Sloane.

"The officer you were dancing with—"

Elizabeth shuddered and wrapped her arms around her waist.

Pierce took her elbow and guided her to the balcony.

"Lizzy." Mary and Jane rushed to her side.

"You were quite correct, Mr. Pierce," Elizabeth whispered. "These officers are uncouth. I should very much like to go home now."

"I will call for your carriage." Mr. Pierce bowed and left.

"What happened?" Jane touched Elizabeth's arm.

"I have never been spoken to in such a way." Elizabeth forced back nausea. "I want to bathe." She hid her face in her hands.

"What of Lydia?" Mary asked.

"She is safer with the Forsters. The officers, it seems, all know Papa is away. I fear they are encouraged to greater boldness in his absence. But, I do not imagine a man like Major Sloane would approach her with his colonel watching."

"I will get Kitty." Jane squeezed Elizabeth's arm and disappeared inside.

In a quarter of an hour, the carriage pulled up, and Mr. Pierce handed them inside. Kitty's exuberant chatter entertained Mary and Jane on the drive. Elizabeth's conversation with Sloane played too loudly in her ears for her to attend anything else.

Later, alone in her bed, she tossed and turned, unable to stop the skin-crawling sensation every remembrance of Sloane evoked. Was a bath possible this late? No, Mama would surely hear the commotion, and disturbing Mama would not improve her situation.

Near dawn, she relinquished the quest for sleep. She slipped into a morning dress, pilfered a snack from the kitchen and curled up in Papa's favorite chair in his study. With the lap blanket that smelled of him firmly tucked around her and her senses full of everything warm and comfortable and safe, her eyes drooped shut and she slept.

CHAPTER 8

Elizabeth forced her eyelids open. The sun beat mercilessly through the window. If the aches throughout her bones were any indication, she had slept past breakfast and quite possibly lunch. The big leather chair had not been designed for sleeping.

"Lizzy! Lizzy!"

Elizabeth pushed the study door open and peeked out.

"You gave us such a fright." Mary peered into Elizabeth's face. "We found your bed empty."

Elizabeth wiped sleep from her eyes. "I could not sleep, so I visited with Papa's books and fell asleep in his chair." She yawned and stretched.

"You found her. Finally." Kitty appeared at Mary's shoulder. "We need your help, Lizzy."

"Please, tell me you did not try to milk the cow yourselves." Elizabeth squeezed her temples. Her stomach churned. Too little sleep, too little dinner and too many officers.

"My goodness, no." Kitty looked at Mary and laughed. "I am too afraid she will kick me."

Mary lifted her hands. "I do not wish to get too close to that hairy beast, either."

"Did the hens attack you as you tried to steal their eggs?" Their bemused expressions were so dear. At least she still made them laugh.

"Please, Lizzy, be serious." Mary pulled her down the hall. "We need you in the kitchen. Little Bonnie Clay is sobbing herself hoarse, and we cannot get her calm enough to tell us what happened."

"I found her near the dairy barn this morning and brought her here." Kitty scurried after them.

"You need Jane—"

"Jane is already away on calls. You are good with children." Mary pushed open the kitchen door.

Bonnie, usually a bundle of energy and sunshine, huddled on a stool, a broken-stemmed daisy after a storm. Hill stood beside her and scolded.

Elizabeth winced. Hill's tongue-lashings caused tears, not relieved them. She nodded a dismissal to Hill. With much patience and a plate of shortbread, she dried Bonnie's tears and coaxed her to talk.

"I went to town to sell the milk, just like Papa told me." Bonnie used her sleeve to wipe her nose.

Kitty handed her a dishcloth.

Bonnie rubbed her cheeks, stared down at the cloth and wadded it in both hands.

"What happened?" Elizabeth crouched beside the stool.

Bonnie wrung the dishcloth into a tight knot. "Coming across the footbridge, coming straight home as I ought." Tears welled, and she trembled. "Billy Thompson. Billy…he"

Elizabeth wrapped her arm across Bonnie's shoulder and whispered, "You are safe now. Tell us what happened. No one will be angry at you."

Kitty twisted the corner of her apron around her fingers and shifted her weight from one foot to the other.

Bonnie looked up at Elizabeth. Tears dripped off her cheeks. "Yes, Miss." She covered her face with her hands and mumbled, "He told me to give him some money, or he wouldn't let me pass. I didn't want to. He scared me, so I…I did. When I…I got to the barns, I knew Papa would see I didn't have enough money, and he would whip me. I hid." She sobbed into the dishcloth.

Elizabeth pushed herself off the floor.

Kitty shrugged and glanced toward the door.

Mary touched Kitty's arm. "Would you tell Hill Lizzy and I will be—"

Kitty rushed toward the door.

"—out for a while."

Just as well. Kitty would not do well on this sort of errand. Elizabeth patted Bonnie's back. "We will talk to your father, Bonnie, and see to Master Thompson as well."

118

Another piece of shortbread comforted the little girl enough to leave the kitchen.

Though Bonnie dragged her feet the entire way, they still arrived at the barns in less than a quarter hour. They found Mr. Clay, a rugged wall of a man with weathered skin and a booming voice, instructing his son, a miniature of himself, on the care of calves. He melted at his daughter's tears, boosting her to his hip so she could bury her face in his shoulder.

Mary and Elizabeth explained Bonnie's story. Clay's eyes blazed dangerously. Without a word, he led the way to the Thompson's. Elizabeth and Mary ran to keep up with his furious pace. No one meddled with Clay's only daughter.

To their great fortune, Mr. Pierce stood with Mr. Thompson in the lane in front of the Thompson's house.

Papa had admonished her to call for Pierce if she encountered tenant problems. Thank Providence, he was already here.

Mary's inquisition quickly penetrated ten-year-old Billy's bravado and extracted his confession. Elizabeth declared the boy should pay back double what he stole, and he could find a position with Mr. Clay in Longbourn's barns. Pierce kept the angry fathers from fisticuffs and mediated until everyone agreed it a fitting balance of accountability and compassion.

"Might I escort you back to Longbourn?" Mr. Pierce asked as the Clays took their leave.

"Thank you, yes." Elizabeth nodded to the Thompsons, waved the Clays on ahead, and followed Mary and Pierce.

The lane offered little shade. Sweat and dust fit perfectly with Elizabeth's already prickly mood.

Pierce offered Mary his arm. "How did you find out?"

"Kitty found Bonnie crying. We needed a whole plate of shortbread to coax the story from her." Mary nestled her hand in the crook of his elbow.

"Excellent stuff to extract a confession, especially your Mrs. Hill's." He chuckled. "I am impressed with the way you resolved this. I think you quite correct in your assessment of young Master Thompson. He will be much better for a little hard work and guidance." He chewed the inside of his cheek.

"I hope so." Elizabeth watched Bonnie struggle to keep up with her father's long strides. "I pray we have done enough."

"If you do not object, I will check in on his progress from time to time. Mr. Clay is a good man and does not have a resentful temper. He will be an excellent influence on the boy." He exhaled heavily. "I fear Billy is one of a number of young men who need such guidance."

"The officers?" Mary asked.

Elizabeth bit her lower lip, brows drawn together. What could Pierce possibly say more alarming than what they witnessed last night? Trickles of sweat trailed down the back of her neck.

Pierce nodded. "Your sister still stays with the colonel and his wife?"

"Yes, sir. We expect she will stay until the regiment departs for Brighton." Elizabeth held her breath.

"I am relieved." He glanced from Mary to Elizabeth.

"Relieved?" Mary's eyes widened.

"Last night after you left, I chanced to hear two young officers discussing, in most vulgar terms, their plans to elope with their sweethearts, tonight. I immediately feared for your sister's wellbeing, but the conversation did not mention her name. Since she stays with the colonel himself, I am certain she is safe." He smiled at Mary. The tense furrows in his forehead eased. "Once I see you to Longbourn, I will pay a visit to those families whose daughters I heard mentioned last night. I do not know if my intelligence will be welcome; nonetheless, my conscience insists I not keep it to myself."

"Far better than taking a chance with a young woman's future." Mary pressed his hand on her arm. "We are so close to the house, you should make haste and visit them now."

"You are, of course, correct." He stopped and bowed. "Thank you, Miss Mary."

They watched him take the narrower path. His pace increased as he went. Their path turned slightly, now dappled with welcome shade.

A breeze raised goose bumps on the back of Elizabeth's neck. "He asked Papa for permission to court you." She arched her brow, head cocked.

Mary's cheeks colored prettily, and she nodded.

"Yet you said nothing."

"We have no need to draw attention to ourselves. We will not deny our courtship to any who asks." Mary walked a little faster.

"You mean you did not want to upset Lydia since she will not be the first to catch a husband." Elizabeth hurried to catch up.

"With Mama indisposed, I could not bring more upset into the household. Mama becomes most distressed when Lyddie is unhappy."

Elizabeth struggled to catch a glimpse of Mary's face. "You sacrifice the opportunity to be Mama's favorite—"

"I do not need to be her favorite—"

"Do you not ever wish for it, just a little?"

Mary kicked a small rock and slowed her pace slightly. "Once in a while. The subject is hard to avoid. Her favorites are so pronounced."

Elizabeth chewed her lip, chest tightening. Jane and Lydia were Mama's favorites; Elizabeth, Papa's; Aunt Phillips doted on Kitty. No one favored Mary. How lonely to be so forgotten. Another nugget of guilt settled next to its sisters under her ribs.

Mary adjusted her bonnet. "I choose to be content as I am. Truly, I have nothing to repine."

"I am happy for you." Elizabeth touched her arm. "And I am glad you will be the first among us to be well settled. He is a good man, and you are well suited."

"We are not engaged yet, Lizzy."

"You will be though."

Mary's shoulders sagged, and the blush faded from her cheeks. "Not if Lydia does something stupid."

How desolate Mary sounded. Elizabeth shook her head. "Then I am not the only one alarmed by what Mr. Pierce heard?"

"I am very worried too."

Elizabeth paused, her hand on the doorknob. "Last night, I agreed with Mr. Pierce that Colonel Forster's protection would be enough."

"But with such radical plans in place—"

"Exactly." Elizabeth opened the door. Anxiety danced a jig in her belly.

Kitty met them at the foyer. "What happened? You must tell me. No, wait, let me get Jane, and you can tell us together. I told her what happened, and she is as anxious as I to hear what transpired." Kitty disappeared up the stairs.

Kitty and Jane joined them on their way to the parlor. Elizabeth related the entire episode before they sat down.

"I wonder which families Mr. Pierce visits." Kitty rubbed her knuckle across her lips.

"I neither know, nor do I want any part in gossip." Mary's eyes narrowed into a glare.

"You do not need to lecture me." Kitty's hands flew to her hips.

Jane patted Kitty's knee and looked deeply into Mary's face. "Mary, what is wrong?"

Mary stared at her feet.

"You do not think the colonel—" Jane said.

"She managed to talk Mrs. Forster into that debacle of a dinner party last night." Elizabeth sprang to her feet and stalked to the window. "Colonel Forster told me I ought to let her have some harmless fun."

"Harmless?" Mary gasped, color draining from her cheeks.

Jane pressed clasped hands to her lips. "Heaven forbid."

Kitty squirmed in her chair and looked away.

"Kitty?" Mary leaned toward her.

Kitty wrung her hands. "Last night I heard her joke—she said what a good laugh it would be for her to return from her visit with Mrs. Forster married herself."

Jane fell back against her chair, pale as Mama's best china.

Elizabeth shuddered and stalked to her sisters. "I will go to pay a visit to the Forsters, now."

"Do you wish me to go with you?" Mary trembled as she pushed up from her seat.

"No, you need to be here in case Lydia should appear here. If she does, keep her here, even if you must tie her to a chair."

Kitty tittered.

Elizabeth whirled on her. "I am not joking."

"You do not need to be harsh with me. I have not done anything so very wrong." Kitty snorted. "Why do you take Lydia's improper behavior out on me?"

Elizabeth threw her head back and sighed. She did not need another battlefront right now. "I am sorry for my harshness. I worry what Lydia's thoughtlessness might cost us all."

"Reserve your anger for her." Kitty turned her back to her sisters.

"Please, forgive us, Kitty." Jane squeezed her shoulder.

Kitty shrugged and grumbled something under her breath.

"Will you go to Lucas Lodge and ask Charlotte and Maria if they know anything of Lydia's intentions?" Jane nudged Kitty with her elbow.

"Do you believe it necessary, or are you trying to get me out of the way?" Kitty's narrow eyes focused directly on Elizabeth.

Elizabeth crossed the distance to Kitty. "Maria spent much time in Lydia's company last night. Talking to her is an excellent thought."

Kitty's expression shifted from pouty to defiant to determined. "I will go."

"Thank you." Elizabeth squeezed her hands.

· • ·&·•·&·•·&·•·&·•·

Spring farm tasks demanded all the horses, so Kitty and Elizabeth set out on foot as soon as bonnets and spencers could be found. Long shadows attested to the waning afternoon, and a cool note in the breeze whispered of impending evening. Kitty turned off the main road toward Lucas Lodge. Elizabeth strode like an old hen in the yard on her way to put a younger one in her place. She could not get to Meryton fast enough, which certainly explained why she encountered Bonnie Clay skipping along the road.

"Miss Bennet!" Bonnie ran toward her.

Elizabeth plastered on an agreeable smile and stopped until Bonnie was at her side. "Good afternoon, Miss Clay."

Bonnie giggled.

"Where are you off to this afternoon?" Elizabeth continued her walk at a considerably easier pace.

"I'm on an errand for my mum. I cannot stay long, or she will be cross." She capered beside Elizabeth. "Thank you for not sending the magistrate for Billy."

Elizabeth stopped, her foot hovering inches above the ground. She recovered her composure just before she stumbled.

"I know he done wrong, but…" Bonnie tittered and hid her face in her hands.

"You like him?" Elizabeth dropped to a knee.

Bonnie nodded rapidly. She peeked between her fingers.

Several admonishments flashed through her mind, all more appropriately delivered by the girl's mother, so Elizabeth simply stared.

"Now he will work for my pa for all the spring and summer. I will get to see him nearly every day." She clapped her hands in time as she bounced on her toes.

"You are pleased with this? I thought you feared him."

"Yes… no." She giggled again. "I…I am happy I will get to see him. Oh, I must go or mum will be angry." Bonnie dashed off.

A sick churning knotted the pit of Lizzy's stomach. Foolish, foolish girl, overlooking Billy's inappropriate behavior to fashion him some sort of dark hero. So much like Lydia. The angry hen returned to her former quick pace toward town

Anger and anxiety only carried her so far. Half a mile from town, she slowed to a ladylike stroll. Colonel Forster, atop his bay stallion, came upon her in her most genteel aspect.

"Good afternoon, Miss Bennet." He waved, but made no move to dismount. He guided the horse alongside her. "Did you enjoy yourselves last night? Mrs. Forster enjoyed the company of you and your sisters."

She hated to lie. "A most memorable evening, sir. I am certain we will talk about it for quite some time to come."

"Capital! Capital!"

"In fact, I was on my way to call upon Mrs. Forster."

"Excellent. She will be happy for someone else to recount the evening's events with. She will have worn out even your sister with the topic by now." He chuckled and blotted sweat from his brow with his sleeve. "Would you be so kind as to carry a message to Mrs. Forster for me?"

"Most certainly, sir."

"If you would, simply tell her I must attend a meeting that will likely last well into the night and will not be home to dine tonight. Getting an entire regiment on the move takes planning." He resettled his hat and winked.

"Will you be meeting with *all* your officers?" She bit her lip, unable to breathe.

"No, just my senior staff. Little point in muddling with the junior men without a plan in place." He bowed from his shoulders. "Very obliging of you to convey my message. Must be off now. Good day." He kicked his horse and disappeared around a bend.

He would not be at home, and his junior officers would have no supervision. Colonel Forster might as well sanction the elopements directly and save them the trouble of sneaking away. Anger and anxiety fueled her pace once more.

•✤✤•✤✤•✤✤•✤✤•✤✤••

By the time Elizabeth reached the Forster's, her heart pounded as though she had run the entire distance to Meryton. She stared at the front door. The normal calling hours had long since come and gone, not that Mrs. Forster would be aware of such niceties. She bit her tongue. A judgmental attitude would not be helpful now. She rapped at the door.

The housekeeper, a weary-looking woman whose stained apron matched her dingy mobcap, let her into the foyer to wait. Elizabeth peeked through open doorways. Neither the dining room nor the makeshift ballroom were fully restored to order. Strange, surely the colonel would want his house back in order immediately. The housekeeper shuffled into the foyer and summoned her to the front parlor. They dodged oddly placed chairs and tables along the way.

Such disarray. Mrs. Forster barely managed her own household, and certainly exerted no control over Lydia. If Elizabeth could just bring Lydia home…she would also be able to part the Thames with just a word. She had to find a way to stay here and keep watch.

"Lizzy!" Lydia shouted. "You see—I told you they would come to call." She flashed a sassy grin at Mrs. Forster.

"You are most welcome, Miss Elizabeth." Mrs. Forster gestured to a chair a most proper hostess mask painted on her face. Her twinkling eyes and twitching lips and belied the oh-so-proper effect.

"What a splendid dinner last night." Lydia hugged herself. "Ever so many people told us a large gathering could not be managed with so little time. We showed them. I cannot wait to arrange the next dinner at Longbourn."

Whilst Lydia's attitude remained unchanged, at least her dress had been. Now, with no witnesses, she wore a proper, and even modest gown.

"What a treasure you have in Lydia." Mrs. Forster patted Lydia's arm. "You would do well to have her—"

This line of conversation had to stop. "Pray excuse me." Elizabeth choked back more pointed words. Each one left a bitter tang on her tongue. "I encountered Colonel Forster on my way here. He asked me to tell you he expected to be in a meeting long into the evening and will not be able to dine with you tonight."

Mrs. Forster huffed, her lips shaped into a practiced, Lydia-like pout. "He plans our move to Brighton. I hate moving so often. Every time I start to enjoy the society of a place, we must uproot and settle elsewhere."

"My poor, dear, Harriet. You are so put upon." Lydia caught Mrs. Forster's hands. "I shall write my father and insist he allow me to travel with you to Brighton."

"What a marvelous thought. Would he would permit it?" Mrs. Forster covered her mouth and turned wide eyes on Elizabeth.

Elizabeth coughed away her more colorful response in favor of, "I think Mama will soon need her at home."

"La! What a goose you are, Lizzy. With four of you at home, Mama does not need me. She would tell me to enjoy myself. I am sure Papa will—"

Elizabeth gripped the arms of her chair. The threadbare fabric separated under her fingers. The stuffing prickled under her nails. She drew a deep breath and forced her hands loose. "Do not be so quick—"

"You are such a bore." Lydia rolled her eyes. "At least you can make yourself useful here and help us to fix the dining room before dinner."

"Excuse me?" Elizabeth's forehead knotted so tightly her temples throbbed.

"The room is in confusion. We need help to restore it." Lydia tossed her head. "The servants have too much work to do today and will not be able to finish before tomorrow. At least that is what we are told."

Elizabeth stared at Mrs. Forster. Did she not recognize Lydia's thoughtlessness? Heat prickled her cheeks. "With the colonel away for dinner—"

"You do not think I believe him, do you?" Mrs. Forster laughed and rose. "No, silly girl, he is just as likely to come home for dinner tonight as any other night. He sends such messages quite often. I ignore them. A number of his officers may come to dine as well. We must get the room in order."

"Since you are here, Lizzy, you can be a proper guest and offer your assistance." Lydia pulled Elizabeth to her feet.

Too stunned for words, Elizabeth allowed Lydia to drag her to the dining room. Lydia spent the next hour ordering Elizabeth to move furniture, dust and polish as though she were a scullery maid. No wonder Kitty believed Lydia thought her a lady's maid. The next hour, Lydia directed the placement of ornaments and linens.

Lydia enjoyed commanding her troops far too much. Mrs. Forster intervened before Lydia launched into a third hour and declared the room finished. They returned to the parlor. Elizabeth fell into a chair, exhausted. The furious walk into Meryton and hours of hard labor took their toll. She could hardly lift her head.

Though late, Mrs. Forster called for tea. "I think we deserve some refreshment." She straightened her skirt. "I am grateful for your help, Miss Elizabeth."

"She was not so very helpful at all. No, Lizzy, do not look at me that way. You know it is true. You did naught but argue where to place the furniture and how to arrange the crystal. I am not sure why you insisted on helping in the first place." Lydia snorted.

Elizabeth closed her eyes. Scolding Lydia right now would require too much effort.

"Lydia, be kind," Mrs. Forster said. "I am sure we would not have finished without your sister's help even if she does not like where I placed the sideboard."

Not yet. A few more moments and Elizabeth would regain enough strength to consider a response. Besides, she still had to obtain an invitation to spend the night, and offending her hostess would not further her ends. The door rattled, and Elizabeth cracked her eyes open.

A young maid entered with a tea service and a meager plate of biscuits. Mrs. Forster clinked and sloshed her way through tea preparation.

Elizabeth took a sip from a less than clean teacup and winced. Mrs. Forster did not realize she had bought used tea leaves. She set the insipid cup aside and examined the biscuits. Irregular and burnt, she would forego those as well.

That left conversation to fill the space between them. "Mrs. Forster, how long have you been married?"

Mrs. Forster glanced at Lydia and giggled. "Six months now. I am the first of my sisters to marry, you know. They were ever so jealous of me when I ordered all the things I would need as the wife of a *colonel*. Sadly, we did not elope."

Lydia sighed. "What a disappointment."

Elizabeth's face turned cold. She choked on the biscuit crumbs left in her mouth.

"I wanted to disappear off into the night and return to announce myself as Mrs. Forster to all my friends and family. Alas, it was not to be."

Elizabeth coughed frantically, choking on words and crumbs, neither of which a panicked gulp of tea washed away.

"Why ever did he refuse you?" Lydia asked.

"Though he proclaimed his love for me, he insisted a respectable husband made sure his wife had a proper settlement and proper wedding witnessed by her proper family and friends. We were wed very properly." Mrs. Forster sipped her tea and pouted. "I am sure you are pleased, Miss Elizabeth, as you seem to be a proper sort yourself."

"I should think your mother and father quite preferred to see you married from your home, with proper settlements in place." Elizabeth dabbed her lips with her napkin, happy to have regained her voice, in spite of the burn in the back of her throat.

"Exactly what I would expect you to say." Lydia harrumphed and bounced on the worn-out settee.

"Without a settlement, a woman has no protection for her or her children if anything happens to her husband. Not even an assurance of pin money, which would be very significant to you, Lydia." Elizabeth crossed her arms tightly and glowered.

"You are completely missing the point." Lydia rose. "Look at the time. We should call for the coach so you can go home." She started off, presumably in search of someone to call for the carriage.

Elizabeth jumped and nearly knocked the teacup off the table. This would not do. Lydia intended to throw her out. "I walked." She sighed dramatically and leaned into the chair, covering her face with her arm. Desperate moments called for desperate measures.

"You poor, tired dear." Mrs. Forster patted Elizabeth's hand on the way to intercept Lydia at the doorway. "It will be dark soon. You cannot possibly get home before—"

"She is a fast walker; she will be fine." Lydia grabbed Elizabeth and pulled her toward the door. "You should get a move on quickly."

Elizabeth dragged her feet shoulders slumped. She leaned heavily against the back of a chair and panted softly.

"No." Mrs. Forster's voice echoed the tone Colonel Forster used while drilling his men. "Join us for dinner and stay the night. A lady cannot walk alone at night. Return home in the morning."

Lydia drew breath, and her cheeks colored. Mrs. Forster's sharp look cut her off.

"Thank you for the invitation." Elizabeth smiled wearily.

"Aunt Phillips lives a short way from here." Lydia hunched her shoulders and wrapped her arms around her belly. "She may stay there. We are such a merry party, why ruin—"

"No. I said she is to stay, and she will stay." Mrs. Forster shrieked like a tiny hawk. "Stop arguing with me, or you will be the one to ruin our merry party. Go upstairs, rest and restore your good humor. Dinner will not be for at least another hour. Go. Now." She pointed toward the staircase, her arm hovered in the air until Lydia complied.

Elizabeth held the tip of her tongue between her teeth. For the first time in her experience, someone out-fussed Lydia. The moment's novelty, and the knowledge that something had finally gone her way today, held her fixed in her spot. If she moved, or even breathed too loudly, something might go wrong again.

"Let me show you to the extra room upstairs." Mrs. Forster took Elizabeth by the elbow and dragged her upstairs. "A small room, to be sure, but compared to walking alone at night, it is quite a pleasant one."

The room in question was tucked beneath an awkward corner of the roof. The ceiling sloped so much she had to stoop to get to the bed or small corner table. "A very fine room, thank you," Elizabeth said.

Mrs. Forster closed the door. With a hand on the low ceiling, Elizabeth picked her way along the bed to sink onto the cushionless window seat. The room smelled of sweat, old boots and gunpowder—not the most appealing aromas. At least she was here, with Lydia.

Someday she would laugh about this night, probably with Papa, by the fire in his study. He would remind her of how she overreacted and suffered Mrs. Forster's hospitality. She would blush under his tease and confess he had known best all along.

Until then, she would endure used tea leaves, tasteless food, boorish company and this Spartan little closet.

CHAPTER 9

An hour later, a fuss at the front door drew Elizabeth out of her room. Well past sundown, with too few candles to light the corridor, long shadows obscured her vision and demanded cautious steps.

"Mrs. Forster."

"Colonel!" Mrs. Forster flew past Elizabeth and down the stairs. "I told them you would come." She extended her hands to her husband.

"So I have. Will you be able to accommodate dinner guests?" He took her hands and smiled broadly.

Elizabeth picked her way down the stairs. She dodged the basket of linens and an empty crock but kicked the wooden box left along the stairs' edge.

"We held dinner in case you and your fine officers might join us after all. I will give word, and we will eat in a quarter hour."

Elizabeth peered over Mrs. Forster's shoulder. Major Sloane, a captain she did not know, Lt. Carter and Lt. Denny milled in the foyer. Bitterness filled her mouth, and the world swayed under her feet. She clutched the creaky banister that threatened to dislodge from the wall. A rutting cony[24] and his foul apprentice to share the table tonight. What a fitting accompaniment for cook's tasteless offerings.

Surely though, the threat of Colonel Forster's ire, backed by the force of military discipline, would dissuade even the most determined rake. Even so, dinner promised to be an unpleasant ordeal. What she must endure for the sake of Lydia's safety.

Half an hour later, the entire party sat at the dining table. The sparse candelabras struggled to light the room. With neither mirror nor polished metal to reflect from, the room remained bathed in shadows. Just as well. If last night's dinner party gave any indication, the food would be a uniform shade of bland and the diners blessed not to have to look at it.

Sloane seated himself next to Elizabeth. His eyes fondled her. One more advantage of the poor light. His lecherous gazes lost potency in the shadows, not enough to set her mind at ease, but enough that she did not flee the table in search of a bath.

"I expected leftovers from last night." Colonel Forster stood to carve the joint and serve the ladies on

---

[24] Cony: mature rabbit

his right and left. "Yet you present us with fresh, hot food, my dear. I am impressed."

Mrs. Forster blushed. "The gentle folk of Meryton have an appetite to rival an entire regiment. Not a scrap of meat nor a crust of bread remained."

"A lovely evening you gave us, madam." Lt. Denny grinned, his focus on Lydia, not Mrs. Forster. "A toast to your hospitality." He lifted his glass. "And your excellent assistance as well, Miss Lydia."

Both ladies tittered.

Elizabeth struggled not to roll her eyes.

"You are a fortunate man indeed, Colonel." Sloane wiped a dab of sauce from his mustache. "All the beauty of Meryton is ensconced within your walls tonight, with Mrs. Forster and her two fair friends." His elbow strayed and rested against Elizabeth's arm.

She edged away and scrubbed her napkin along her forearm.

"I do believe you are correct." Colonel Forster beamed at his wife.

Sloane's boot touched her foot. Elizabeth jumped. "How go your plans for the regiment's transfer to Brighton?" She focused on the colonel despite Sloane's leer that raised the hairs on the back of her neck.

"Well enough, I suppose. I doubt you can appreciate the logistics involved." Forster winked and his men laughed. "They are complex for a woman to grasp—"

Elizabeth gritted her teeth until her jaw throbbed.

"Lizzy thinks she is just as smart as you, Colonel." Lydia's shoulders bounced in time with her words.

All the men snickered.

Blood rushed to Elizabeth's cheeks. They prickled and stung with the heat.

"I have heard of your cleverness, Miss Bennet, but do not tax yourself to understand this business. Suffice to say, we have it well in hand."

Elizabeth plastered a hollow smile across her lips and blinked her scowls away. Colonel Forster might as well have patted her on the head. Would he identify her as the culprit if she kicked him under the table?

Nothing improved during the second course. Dry fish sauced with inane jokes. Over-stewed cucumbers steeped in empty remarks concerning the weather. Burnt potatoes seasoned by shallow opinions and meager information.

Only the not so subtle glances and smiles Lydia and Lt. Denny exchanged across the table prevented Elizabeth from excusing herself. To miss those clues might spell disaster. She studied and catalogued each one through the soggy pastry and sour fruit that the Forsters' cook called a pie.

Mrs. Forster led the ladies to the drawing room. A pot of tasteless tea and crumbling shortbread awaited them.

"What a wonderful evening. Can you not get Colonel Forster to change his mind and join us? It is dreadfully unfair of him to keep his officers holed up in the dining room discussing business." Lydia dropped into a most unladylike posture on the chair nearest the fireplace. Her head lolled, and she threw her arm over her face. "Lord, I am so fagged."[25]

"And well you should be. We all worked hard today." Mrs. Forster picked up a piece of shortbread that crumbled in her hand before she got it to her mouth. The crumbs fell to her plate. She dropped the dish on the side table with a heavy sigh. "My husband will not be moved."

"Since the gentlemen will not join us, perhaps we should retire?" The torment had continued long enough. Another hour with insipid company and Elizabeth would be a candidate for Bedlam. How to persuade Lydia?

Lydia straightened and looked directly at Elizabeth. "That is the first smart thing you have said all afternoon. We should all retire."

Mrs. Forster yawned deeply. "I must escort you all upstairs ahead of me. A proper hostess cannot be the first to retire."

"You are everything proper, Harriet." Lydia giggled.

Like a wrong chord in a familiar melody, Lydia's laughter rang off key. Elizabeth's stomach clamped down on her paltry dinner. The flavor did not improve a second time around. What inspired Lydia's uncharacteristic agreeableness? Surely not a change of heart.

---

[25] Fagged: tired, drained, exhausted

Mrs. Forster held a sputtering tallow candle and led them through the obstacles on the stairs to their rooms.

The tiny, awkward chamber provided Elizabeth no more comfort now than earlier in the day. She knocked her head on the impractical ceiling twice in attempts to view the street clearly from the window. Her view remained blocked by inconsiderate architecture and insufficient funds for proper glazing. This would not do at all. She tidied her dress, wrapped a borrowed shawl around her shoulders and returned to the parlor.

The fireplace still crackled with a warm fire. Books on the shelves beside the fireplace promised she might spend a tolerable evening. She picked two books, both romantic novels. Not her preferred choice, but Mrs. Forster would no more keep philosophy or poetry than Lydia would conduct herself with Jane's poise and decorum. *Oh, Lydia.*

Elizabeth settled into a lumpy chair and read the first several chapters of *The Mysteries of…*something or other. The title hardly mattered. By the third chapter, she skimmed the text, and by the sixth, brazenly skipped pages all together. How anyone might be entertained by such…such…

"Miss Elizabeth?"

She jumped. Colonel Forster stood in the doorway. "I hope we have not disturbed your repose." He glanced over his shoulder.

"Not at all, sir. I did not hear you pass." She folded the novel shut in her lap.

"Remind me never to ask you to stand watch. The French could kill us all in our sleep, and you would never notice." He winked.

"I will save my money to buy a substitute should I ever be selected for the Hertfordshire militia." She bowed her head.

He threw his head back and laughed. "Very wise. I am for Bedfordshire[26] myself. I wish you a pleasant evening." He bowed and tramped up the stairs.

A door closed upstairs. She hurried to the window and peeked outside. Three men still stood in front of the house. Denny, Sloane and Carter. She stayed at the window until they rode away.

Why did her anxiety not leave with them? Chill bumps rose along her arms. She scrubbed them off. They stubbornly reappeared on her scalp and refused to be scratched away.

She returned to the novel. The melodrama might somehow drown out her dread. Somewhere between the death of—was it Randolph?—and page four hundred and thirty five, she drifted off to sleep.

⋅•᷐᷎⋅•⋅᷐᷎⋅•⋅᷐᷎⋅•⋅᷐᷎⋅•⋅᷐᷎•⋅

Two off key gongs announced the wee hours of the morning.

Elizabeth jumped and shook the fog from her mind. How long? Long enough—Lydia? She sprang for the stairs.

---

26 I am for Bedfordshire: I am going to bed

A hushed snicker and footfalls from the darkness stopped her. Blood roared in her ears. Blast it all, she needed to hear. The crock bounced down the stairs and shattered on the tile.

"Oops." More giggling.

Elizabeth's heart pounded hard enough to break a rib.

Lydia appeared at the bottom of the stairs, breathless, a bag in each hand. She whisked through the foyer to throw open the front door.

"Denny!" Lydia cried.

He shushed her and reached for her bags.

She clapped a hand over her mouth and tittered through her fingers.

Cold terror covered Elizabeth's face and moved into her lungs. Why would her feet not move?

"Hurry, Forster might wake." Denny grabbed Lydia's elbow.

She stumbled and tripped. He dropped one of the bags to catch her.

Elizabeth gasped and lurched forward. "Lydia."

"Lizzy?" The darkness masked Lydia's expression. She pushed Denny toward the door. They both tried to force through at the same time only to tangle against each other. After a second attempt, they made it through.

"Lydia, stop!" Elizabeth ran to the doorway.

A gig waited in the shadows. Denny and Lydia dashed toward it.

Elizabeth screamed until her voice gave way.

The couple paused, looked at her, and sprinted for the gig. Lydia struggled to climb in. Denny grabbed her by the waist to boost her to the seat.

Elizabeth ran into the street.

Denny threw Lydia's bags onto the seat and scrambled up. He gathered the reins and slapped the horse.

The shawl fluttered in the wind and slipped off Elizabeth's shoulder. She caught it before the breeze carried it away. Like a madwoman, she ran for the horse, screaming and flapping the shawl.

The confused animal whinnied and shied. The gig pushed backward a few feet.

Denny flicked his whip. "Damn it, you! Stop that!"

Elizabeth slid on a pile the horse had left behind and fell hard.

"Gi-up!" Denny snapped the reins.

The horse snorted, pawed the ground and took a tentative step.

"What the bloody hell is going on?" Colonel Forster's voice boomed.

Lydia screamed.

"Stop right there, Lieutenant." Colonel Forster rushed out in nightshirt and hessians. He hauled Elizabeth to her feet with one hand and seized the horse's bridle with the other.

"Colonel…" Denny and Lydia sputtered simultaneously.

"The fiddle-faddle I heard about eloping—damn!" Colonel Forster braced Elizabeth against the cart and yanked Denny from his perch. He shoved Denny back with a string of colorful invectives.

Elizabeth's gown stank like a barn in need of cleaning. Hill would be beyond words. Perhaps she might want to borrow some of the colonel's language for the occasion.

"Get your worthless arse back to your boarding house. If you ever come sniffing around Miss Lydia again, I swear I will flog you myself, you worthless—" Colonel Forster shoved Denny and sent him sprawling in the dirt.

Elizabeth gulped in a deep breath. She had not breathed for quite some time.

Colonel Forster helped Lydia down. He took her by the shoulders, lifted her onto tiptoes, and shook her hard. "I cannot believe he talked you into an elopement. Damn fool notion. What a disgrace. You are lucky your sister—" He sucked in a gulp of air and slowly released his grasp on Lydia. "Miss Elizabeth, I am deeply in your debt for preventing—and under my roof no less. I cannot offer enough apologies."

One, two, three breaths. "Thank you, sir. I am most grateful for your intervention. Lt. Denny—"

"That man's brains are in his bollocks. Beggin' your pardon, madam." He took Lydia by the elbow. "Come inside, the night air is not good for ladies."

Lydia sputtered and protested to no avail.

He called a maid to assist Elizabeth and demanded Mrs. Forster attend him immediately.

Elizabeth retreated to the tiny room. Still, Forster's tongue lashing reached her as clearly as if she stood with his wife and Lydia. How strange to be thankful for a fall in a dung pile.

The first lights of dawn broke over the horizon. Forster trudged upstairs. Several minutes later, he knocked at Elizabeth's door, properly attired.

"What may be done for your and your sister's comfort?"

"We should return to Longbourn. Immediately." Elizabeth yawned and rubbed her eyes. "We have imposed on you long enough."

"I understand. I will accompany you myself. I regret my wife may have nurtured that foolishness—"

"Lydia made her own choices. I am grateful you arrived when you did." She nodded.

"I will order the carriage." He bowed and left.

In the half hour required to pack and take leave, the coach pulled up at the front door. Lydia climbed in, sniffling.

Elizabeth waited until the door shut, and the coach started off. "How could you be so stupid, so thoughtless, so selfish?"

"We were going to Gretna Green to be married. Married, Lizzy, me, the youngest, the first to marry." Lydia turned aside. "You are jealous. You have no beau. You do not want anyone attending to me."

Elizabeth closed her eyes and sighed. Lydia cast her as the enemy. Nothing she said would matter, so she said nothing.

Papa had been right. The colonel had protected Lydia. Would he have gotten there in time if she had not slowed their escape? She did not know and it did not matter. Lydia was safe.

Hill opened the door for them. Elizabeth raised her hand to stave off questions. "Take Lydia upstairs to her room. Wake Betsy or Mattie to keep watch and ensure she does not sneak out."

Hill curtsied and dragged Lydia upstairs. Elizabeth counted footsteps until the bedroom door closed. She sagged against the wall. Her knees threatened to melt beneath her.

"Lizzy?"

She looked up into Jane's worried face. Mary peeked over her shoulder.

"Did she…" Jane whispered.

"She tried." Elizabeth closed her eyes and let her head drop against the wall.

"How did you get back?" Mary asked.

"The colonel brought us in his coach." A wry smile lifted the corner of her lips. "What, did you think—we walked home?"

"The thought crossed my mind." Jane caught Elizabeth's elbow. "Come, let me help you to bed. You can tell us everything later after you sleep."

"I will help Lydia." Mary turned toward the stairs.

"Thank you." Elizabeth followed Jane. Soon she was tucked in bed and deep in a dreamless sleep.

A shriek pierced the quiet morning air.

Elizabeth sprang from her bed, fully alert. That was Mama's voice! She bolted from her room.

Mama stood in the corridor, pale and trembling. "My dearest girl, my Lydia. We are ruined!"

"Mama, what is wrong?" Elizabeth clutched Mama's arm. The clock in the hall read nearly noon. Time enough for Lydia to have done something utterly stupid.

"The elopements, my Lydia…" Mrs. Bennet sobbed wildly.

Elizabeth rushed for Lydia's room. Her heart raced faster than her feet. She tripped on the hem of her nightgown, caught herself on the wall, staggered several steps and bounced against the door with her shoulder. After several attempts, she threw it open.

Lydia stood on the other side. "La! What a fuss so early in the morning." A loud yawn and deep stretch followed.

Elizabeth grabbed her hand and hauled her into the hallway. "She is here, Mama."

Mrs. Bennet trundled toward them. "My dearest girl." She fell, weeping, on Lydia's neck.

"We fetched her home last night," Elizabeth whispered.

"Mama!" Jane, Mary and Kitty tumbled into the hallway.

Jane led Mama and Lydia to Mama's room. Mary and Kitty helped Elizabeth to hers.

"Where did Mama hear of elopements?" Elizabeth sank onto her bed.

"She must have overheard." Kitty turned to Mary.

"Maria Lucas called—" Mary pressed her lips tightly.

Elizabeth scoured her face with her hands. What disaster had taken place while she slept?

"She brought the most astonishing news." Kitty bounced down next to her. "Olivia Bond eloped with Lt. Carter last night. Her father left early to catch them before they get to Gretna Green. Even if he does, they still must marry. Little good it did them cutting us." She snorted.

"Poor stupid, stupid, girl." Elizabeth covered her eyes.

"No doubt Lydia intended to do the same," Mary said.

"It was at the hand of Providence I woke when I did." Elizabeth peeked through her fingers. "I nearly missed the whole thing."

Jane poked her head in and sat on Elizabeth's other side. "God has been very good to us. I shudder to think the effect on Mama had Lydia eloped."

Elizabeth groaned. "I cannot imagine."

Mary leaned on the bedpost. She toyed with the fringe along the edge of the bed curtain. "Which of us do you reckon best to take Lydia to task for this?"

"There is no need." Jane smiled.

Mary tossed the bed curtain aside. "You can hardly be so naïve as to think—"

"No, no. Mama already speaks to her." Jane's eyes widened, and she shrugged. "I believe seeing Lydia safe at home rallied her spirits. When I left them, Mama had just said, 'I am so glad you did not elope, my dear, for the disgrace would keep me from seeing you ever again. You would not be welcomed at Longbourn for the rest of your life. I do not know how I would bear it.'"

"She said that?" Kitty covered her mouth with her hands. "What did Lydia do?"

"She turned very pale and quiet. Mama's sternness surprised her," Jane said.

"I never imagined Mama to be the one to talk sense into her. That is Providence for sure." Elizabeth laughed with them until they all wept tears of relief.

CHAPTER 10

Two weeks of persistent storms kept them all at home. Lydia mourned the muddy roads and wet skies that prevented her from seeing the regiment's departure. Though Elizabeth detected some small reformation in Lydia's character, great change required more time. Mama, still shaken by the elopement, worked on her daily, so Elizabeth maintained hope.

The first clear day, Elizabeth seized the opportunity to visit Mrs. Clay. The farmer's wife would not concern herself with Elizabeth's muddy petticoats.

"Thank you kindly for your visit, Miss Bennet." Mrs. Clay still held the package Elizabeth had brought.

"I hope Bonnie feels better soon. The cherry bark should help. I will inform Papa of the storm damage to the roof as soon as he returns." Elizabeth picked up her now empty basket and took her leave.

The afternoon sun, already at work on the muddy road, beat upon her. Hints of summer filled the woods. Bright red berries decorated the berry patch. She needed to tell Hill. Canning season would be upon them in a few weeks, less perhaps. She paid little attention as she walked home. Her feet knew the way along the familiar paths.

Papa would be home soon. His letter said Uncle Gardiner and a guest would join him. Mama's nerves did not permit overnight guests often. What could Papa mean by bringing two?

"You there! Pray excuse me."

"Who calls me?" She squinted into the woods.

"I am lost," an unfamiliar young man called from the middle of the berry bushes. He fought his way toward her through the brambles.

"Have you a name, sir?" She edged backwards. He did not appear menacing. On the contrary, the well-dressed man wore a most bemused expression.

"Forgive me, madam. With no one to make a proper introduction, I am left to introduce myself. Fitzwilliam Darcy of Pemberley in Derbyshire." He bowed slightly and caught his coat on a thorny cane. He fumbled to release the snag.

He sported good diction and an even better tailor.

"I am pleased to meet you, Mr. Darcy of Pemberley." She curtsied. "I am Miss Elizabeth Bennet of Longbourn, the estate you trespass upon."

"Please forgive my trespass, Miss Bennet." The last of the branches released him, and he stumbled onto the path near her.

"How have you come to be lost in my father's woods, so far from the main road?" She crossed her arms and arched her brow. Attractive, well-mannered men rarely appeared out of nothing.

"We drove a great distance today. I left my friend at the cottage not far from here to visit with—" He scratched his head and glanced over his shoulder.

"Mr. Pierce?"

"Yes." He resettled his hat. "That was the name."

She relaxed slightly. "He is the curate in this parish and my father's tenant. We hold him in high regard."

He stared into her eyes for slightly longer than strictly proper, but with none of the distasteful effects of Sloane's gazes.

"You were telling me how you came to be in the woods, sir." She smiled archly.

He shook his head and blinked. "Ah, yes. I needed to stretch my legs, so I decided to walk to town and sent my driver ahead. I saw a small path off the road and followed it."

"You became distracted by the loveliness of our woods and, before you knew, you lost your way." Mama warned her not to tease, especially strangers. But who could resist such a ripe predicament?

He dug his toes into the mud, ears crimson.

Poor man, lost and embarrassed. "I should laugh at your misfortune, but I strive to avoid hypocrisy."

He lifted his head, eyes wide. Dark brown and full of depth, they were riveting.

"Let me help you find your way to the main road." She walked on.

"I am quite in your debt. Usually I am far more observant."

"Long hours in a carriage causes my mind to wander. I am quite sympathetic." She glanced back at him.

"Might I be of service, madam? May I carry that for you?" He reached for the large basket.

"An empty basket is hardly any trouble. You should have lost your way several hours ago if you desired to be truly gallant." She laughed. What a dear, perplexed expression poor Mr. Darcy wore. Probably the eldest son of a very serious man whom no one dared tease.

"What would you bring into the woods in such a large container? This would hold a meal for quite a large family." He held the basket in front of him, turning it this way and that.

"What a forward question for an acquaintance of such short duration." She swatted a stray branch away from her face.

His shoulders fell the barest bit, and his lips pressed his smile away.

This would not do. "My mother tells me I am far too forward myself, and a poor judge of such things, so I will answer you."

Darcy chuckled softly. The most appealing dimple appeared in his right cheek.

"I brought soup and other comforts to two of my father's tenants who are taken with colds."

"Nothing too serious, I hope. We recently lost our previous vicar to a cold that settled into his lungs. I traveled here with our new vicar."

"So your friend recently became vicar?" Elizabeth peeked at him. If she were not careful, she too, would stare.

"Yes, he served as curate for almost all my life and has many friends pleased to see him take the parish." Darcy's voice warmed. "We rely upon his wisdom regularly."

"He sounds like our Mr. Pierce." Mary's Mr. Pierce.

"Does your curate deliver a good sermon?"

"That would depend upon whom you ask. He writes his own sermons, so we have much speculation during the week as to what he will speak about on Sundays."

Darcy snickered. "Forgive me. The last time I encountered my aunt's ridiculous parson, he waxed most philosophical on the sinful arrogance of a man who writes his own sermons. Plato he is not."

Attractive, well-mannered *and* educated. Her heart stumbled through several beats.

"No one may accuse him of dispensing wisdom to his parish. His flock is truly safe from those unsettling influences. I imagine his sermons are also much discussed though for different reasons."

"I quite understand." She pressed her lips tightly. It would not do to expose him to all her impertinence at once. She pointed through a break in the branches.

"We have reached the main road, Mr. Darcy of Pemberley."

"I am in your debt, Miss Bennet of Longbourn." He bowed, a delightful twinkle in his eye. "I hope to make your acquaintance again under more conventional circumstances so we may be properly introduced." He returned her basket.

"I thank you, sir, for the compliment. If your stay here will be of some duration, we will likely meet in town, or perhaps at the upcoming assembly." She curtsied.

"The other friend I traveled with is here to see Netherfield Park in anticipation of taking a lease. Is that property near your father's estate?"

"Yes sir, Netherfield is our nearest neighbor." New tenants at Netherfield. If his friend were like him, that could be a very good thing, indeed. "Does your friend have a wife?"

"His sister will keep house for him."

"My sisters and I will pay her a call soon. Once on the road, a walk of less than an hour will bring you into town."

He stared at her again.

Why did that leave her warm and tingly?

Darcy nodded and ambled away.

A dimpled smile was certainly worth looking at. *Perhaps it is a very good thing Netherfield Park will be let at last.*

DON'T MISS THE EPILOGUE

THE RAWLSES VISIT LONGBOURN

A WEB EXCLUSIVE
AT

GIVENGOODPRINCIPLES.COM

ABOUT THE AUTHOR

Though Maria Grace has been writing fiction since she was ten years old, those early efforts happily reside in a file drawer and are unlikely to see the light of day again, for which many are grateful.

She has one husband, two graduate degrees and two black belts, three sons, four undergraduate majors, five nieces, six cats, seven Regency-era fiction projects and notes for eight more writing projects in progress. To round out the list, she cooks for nine in order to accommodate the growing boys and usually makes ten meals at a time so she only cooks twice a month.

She can be contacted at:
author.MariaGrace@gmail.com.

You can find her profile on Facebook:
facebook.com/AuthorMariaGrace

or visit her website at:
AuthorMariaGrace.com

GOOD PRINCIPLES
P U B L I S H I N G

14101367R00112

Made in the USA
Charleston, SC
21 August 2012

[2]